THE *ex* FILES SERIES

EXILED

LISA RYAN CAMPBELL

Cover design by Deranged Doctor Design
www.derangeddoctordesign.com

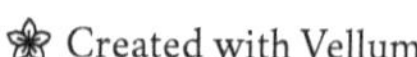 Created with Vellum

That was a gunshot.

Deputy Timothy Caine was fortunate enough to have lived a life where gunshots weren't a common sound growing up, but since joining the sheriff's department, he made sure to visit the range often. In Gypsy Bay, he hadn't been forced to use his service revolver very often, but those trips to the range had caused him to grow accustomed to the sound of that quick lethal pop.

"What the hell?"

He was coming up the hill in the direction of the shot and slowed as he saw the wreckage up ahead. Through the driving sheets of rain, he could see there were two cars. The first didn't look to have any damage from the rear, but the second vehicle had plowed into the railing. A few more feet and it would have fallen below into the rocks and ocean. Maybe a fender bender, but the first car had to have been going very fast to cause the other to crash into the railing. He picked up his radio, called dispatch, and gave the necessary information to send an ambulance to the scene. As he got closer, a woman walked right out in front of his car, causing him to slam on his brakes.

"Dammit! Lady, I almost—"

The rest of that sentence froze in his throat as he realized two things at once: the African-American woman in the black cocktail dress was Shannon Spencer, and she was holding a gun. Timothy put his vehicle in park. With slow, deliberate caution, he climbed out, using one hand to take his service weapon out of its holster.

He spoke loudly above the downpour. "Mrs. Spencer, I'm Deputy Caine. I need you to drop the gun."

She didn't seem to hear him. She just kept staring at him as if in a daze.

"You know me, Mrs. Spencer. You and the sheriff watched my girls play in the softball championship, remember? I'm no threat to you. Now, put the gun down."

She stood rooted to the ground, and even though the gun was at her side, her finger kept teasing the trigger.

"Drop the gun, Shannon!"

His raised voice finally jolted her out of her trance. She looked at the gun in her hand as if she hadn't realized she was holding it, and then slowly put it to the ground. When she spoke, it was with an eerie calmness.

"I can't find my cell phone. Please, call an ambulance."

For the first time, Timothy noticed a body lying face-up beside the car. He took another look and nearly choked when he realized it was his sheriff. He was lying there so still with his face a deathly white and the rain pelting his chest, washing away the blood. Jesus, there was so much blood.

"What happened?" he asked, still keeping his gun trained on her.

"There—there was an accident."

"Is he dead?"

"No," she said, tears streaming down her face. "Please, help him."

"Help is coming," he said, already hearing the distant sound of sirens. "I heard gunfire as I was coming up the hill. Dispatch is already getting calls of shots being fired in this area."

She didn't speak.

He gestured to the car beside him that didn't seem to have any damage. "Whose car is this?"

"Cody's."

"Cody Spencer?"

She nodded.

He should have guessed. Only a guy like Cody would drive around in an electric-blue babe magnet like that.

"Where is he?"

"He fell. Over the cliff."

That stunned him. He looked toward the highway railing and saw nothing but darkness. What the hell happened here? He looked back at Shannon, who continued to remain a statue, standing by her husband's lifeless body. Christ, he didn't want to ask. He did not want to ask. But as his only witness, he needed to get answers from her. Still, this was also the sheriff's wife, and if she said anything to incriminate herself...

"How did that happen?"

She answered him, but he could barely hear her over the whine of the sirens of the EMTs and more sheriff's department vehicles making their way up the hill.

"Shannon, how did Cody fall over the cliff?"

She said it louder this time, and when he heard the words, he wished she had just kept quiet.

"I shot him."

CHAPTER ONE

*F*our years later…

More times than I could count, I'd dreamed about the first thing I would do when I finally left the Central California Women's Facility—scream to the heavens, stoop and kiss the ground, or maybe do a little victory dance. But when that day finally came, it was nothing at all dramatic. I simply walked out, letting the automatic gates shut behind me, effectively trapping the gray and ominous structure that had been my home for the past three years. And I kept walking without looking back.

Marissa's little Volvo wasn't out there, but I smiled when I saw whom she'd sent as her replacement.

Jeremy Barrett, Gypsy Bay's youngest and brightest criminal defense lawyer, stepped from his car and walked around the other side to open the passenger door. I hefted the small duffle bag on my right shoulder carrying everything I brought into the prison with me, and when I reached Jeremy, I dropped it at his feet, laughed, and fell into his arms.

"How've you been?" he asked, once he released me and got a good look at me.

"Is that a trick question?"

He had the grace to wince. "Sorry."

He bent down to pick up my duffle and put it in his trunk before heading to the driver's side.

"How's business?"

He gave a nonchalant shrug, which meant he was busier than he could handle, and then waved his hand, indicating for me to get in.

"Let's get the hell out of here," he said.

I climbed into the car and nearly balked at the leather seating. It was an unusually hot summer day, even for northern California, and it wouldn't be long before my thighs began to sweat and stick to the seat. But I told myself to shut up and just be grateful someone still gave enough of a damn to pick me up in the first place. In reality, it seemed like Jeremy and Marissa were my only two friends in the world, and I would need them—especially when we reached Gypsy Bay. I was certain news of my release had reached the town weeks ago, and the whole town must be awash in gossip.

I turned to Jeremy and thought about asking him what they were saying about me but decided it would be a waste of breath. The man didn't get involved in town gossip, and if he had heard anything vicious about me, he wouldn't say.

"How's Marissa?"

Another shrug. "She's fine, I guess. They were short at the diner tonight, so she asked me to come get you so she could work an extra shift."

"I appreciate it." In the side-view mirror, I could see the walls of the prison fading farther and farther away and began to breathe easier, knowing that no one was coming after us, demanding that I return. It wasn't a dream that I'd been granted early probation. This was for real.

"You need a job, Shannon."

His low but firm tone broke into my thoughts, and I turned to face him. "I know that. As soon as I get back and settled, I'll start looking for one."

A visible frown creased his forehead.

"What?"

"It's going to be difficult. You really think someone's going to be willing to hire you after..."

He trailed off, but I knew what he was about to say. No, I didn't expect anyone to hire me, but I had to try. I knew my probation officer would be calling the minute I gave him a contact number, and a job would be one of the first things he'd ask about.

"I know what I need to do."

"Listen, they need help at Charlie's, and Marissa said she would talk to the manager. You used to work there in high school, so you've got some experience."

"You don't have to take care of me, Jeremy. I'm not your client anymore."

"No, you're not. But I promised myself that, after what happened, I'd look out for you."

I didn't like where this was going. "I hope you don't think I blame you. You did your best for me, despite—"

"Despite the fact that you confessed to murder? Despite the fact that you kept pleading guilty?"

"I was guilty."

His took his eyes off the road for just an instant, and I saw just how angry he was with me, with everything.

"You may be guilty of something, Shannon, but I'll never believe you shot that man in cold blood, and I'm not just saying that because I'm your lawyer. I know you. You haven't changed that much since high school."

"I've changed enough."

He shook his head, obviously frustrated with me, but willing to let the subject drop for the moment.

"Marissa says you'll probably be able to start this weekend if things go well," he said.

I looked away without a reply, assuming that would be answer enough. Of course I was going to take the job if it was offered to me. I just didn't like being dependent on anyone, but that's what three years in prison will do to a girl.

"Why don't you just go ahead and ask me."

I turned back, caught off guard by his softer tone. "Ask you what?"

"Whatever's been on your mind since the moment you found out you were being released."

Silence rested between us for the longest time, and briefly, I decided I was going to ignore the question altogether. But, dammit, I did need to know.

"What are they saying about me?"

"They don't want you there."

I feigned a bitter laugh. "I figured as much. Could you be more specific?"

Jeremy looked over at me and then turned back to the road. The next moment, he swerved his car over to the highway shoulder and put it in park. Then he faced me again, and for the first time, I saw the vulnerable look of a man who knew what unbearable pain was like. Apparently, he'd changed since high school, too.

"I'm not going to lie to you; you're in for a rough time, and I won't repeat some of the things I've been hearing. Everyone is in an uproar about your release." He looked ahead to the road that lay before us for only an instant and then focused on me again. "To tell you the truth, I brought along a few thousand dollars with me. I wanted to give it to you, tell you to take my car, and go start a life somewhere else."

I shook my head. "I wouldn't have taken it from you."

He sighed. "I know that. Your aunt raised you with a

backbone. If people were coming at you with pickaxes and torches, you'd get some of your own."

"You and I both know I'm not going back there to start any trouble."

He scoffed. "Not intentionally."

I smiled at that. "Okay, not intentionally."

I then nodded toward the landscape ahead, and with a loud sigh, he turned back in his seat and hit the gas.

"For what it's worth, Sheriff Spencer is doing everything he can to keep the hate calls at bay."

I looked out the side window again, closing my eyes at the mention of his name.

"Yeah, well, that's our sheriff. Good through and through."

I could sense Jeremy watching me, but I didn't acknowledge him, my mind now consumed with thoughts of what I intended to do when I returned to the sleepy little coastal town I used to call home.

* * *

Jeremy's car pulled into the parking lot of Charlie's at nearly ten minutes to six that afternoon. I hadn't even realized I'd fallen asleep until I woke with a start when he nudged me.

"Come inside and get something to eat," he said. "Then I'll take you home."

I looked toward the diner, saw the small crowd of people inside, and shook my head. "I'll just have a burger, fries, and a soda. Can't you just order that to go?"

He looked toward the diner and then back at me. "You'll have to face these people some time. Might as well be now. Come on; I won't let anything happen to you."

Those words warmed me and gave me the little boost I needed to follow him inside. He was right. Besides, if I was this concerned about people's reactions from seeing me walk into a lousy diner, just wait until they found out I was planning to work there.

But when we entered Charlie's, my apprehension returned. The scene was just like something out of those classic westerns where the entire room got quiet, and all that could be heard was the whistle of the wind. I took one look around the room and cursed under my breath. Screw this; I was waiting in the car.

But Jeremy must have felt my hesitation because he took me by the arm and led me to a barstool at the counter. Immediately upon sitting down, one of the patrons next to me got up, threw his money onto the counter, and strode out. Jeremy paid him no mind but handed me a menu.

"Get whatever you want. I'm going to use the restroom."

Before he left, he gave the entire establishment a stern glance. Soon, servers returned to filling drink orders, and customers went back to their meals and now very hushed conversations.

I eyed the restaurant and was both surprised and glad to see the owner had made improvements to both the interior and exterior. It looked more like a family restaurant, not just some dive bar with a bunch of booths. I also liked that there was more square footage, and with the way the servers were hopping around inside, they needed help. I'd been a good server at eighteen and was sure I could get my rhythm back, as soon as I could get rid of the sense of déjà vu.

I tried to relax, despite the stares I felt at my back, and focus on the menu in front of me. Jeremy warned me, and I wasn't so naïve as to think people had forgiven and forgotten —especially since I was being let go much earlier than expected. Everyone in town cursed the parole board for granting that early release, but I was forever grateful to them. They'd given me the opportunity I needed to return and finish what had been started four years ago. But now, after this cold greeting from such a small group of people, I knew it was going to be harder than I thought.

Soft arms came around and enveloped me from behind. The feeling was so foreign to me that I jerked away on impulse. I turned around and met the warm smile of my oldest and dearest friend.

"Marissa," I said, tears coming to my eyes as I got up from the barstool and embraced her.

"Sorry, I didn't mean to scare you," Marissa said, holding me tightly. She pulled away and looked me up and down.

"Okay, this is not fair at all," Marissa said. "You gained weight, but in all the right places. How is that possible?"

I brushed her away, feeling embarrassed by the compliment, but Marissa grabbed hold of me again and hugged me close.

"I missed you," I said, breathing in the scent of her hair. It was some fruity shampoo, and I suddenly realized how much I'd taken girly things like fruity body wash and lotions for granted.

"Same here. Have you been to the house yet?"

"No. I'm grabbing something to eat, and Jeremy is driving me over later."

Marissa's smile faded as she pulled away. "Have you seen him?"

I knew whom she meant. His presence was felt everywhere, even if he wasn't nearby. "No."

"The selfish side of me is so glad you're here, but…"

"But what?"

Marissa looked around, leaned in closer, and spoke in a whisper. "You should've stayed away, Shannon."

I sighed, turned, and picked up the menu again. "Jeremy said as much to me in the car."

"There are other towns, other cities. Why did you come back?"

I couldn't explain. I couldn't tell my friend that what took place that night four years ago wasn't the end of it and that I'd come back to Gypsy Bay to relive it all.

CHAPTER TWO

I turned the key in the lock, hesitated, and then pushed the door open. I stood there, rooted at the front door, staring into the darkened foyer and deathly afraid to enter my childhood home.

"Shannon?"

I turned to see Jeremy stepping out of his car and then held up a hand to stay him.

"I'm fine."

He gave a slight nod and took his time before returning to his car. I was going to have to brave it, or he would once again insist on seeing me inside.

I felt for the wall switch that was to my left and flipped it on. Amazingly enough, the entryway illuminated with soft light. I turned once again to Jeremy and waved him goodbye, and then stepped inside and shut the front door.

It was a cozy two-story home with a living room, dining area, and kitchen on the bottom floor, and two bedrooms that shared a bathroom on the upper level. I knew this house like the back of my own hand, but being away from it for three years made everything that was once familiar look completely foreign. The death of my parents when I was twelve years old had been a crushing blow to my sense of order and peace. However, Aunt Christine, who'd worked as a manager for one of Gypsy Bay's two grocery stores, had swooped in and done her best to restore the peace I thought I'd lost. Then when she passed, leaving everything to me, her only niece, I just felt lost. After her death, I didn't have the energy to go through everything and sort out what I wanted to keep and donate. One morning, when grief had gotten the best of me, I decided I would just throw everything away, sell the house, and move on with my life.

Gray, with his typical level-headed reasoning, told me to take a year to mourn.

"There's no rush," he'd said. "She left everything to you, and this stuff isn't going anywhere. Take your time. It's what I did when my parents died."

So, I followed his advice and didn't touch anything. By that time, we were married, and I was going through so many mixed emotions with resisting the urge to fall in love with him and regretting the ugly deal I made with Cody, there had been no time to think about anything else. Then Cody had died, I was convicted of manslaughter, and the house and all its belongings sat, waiting for my return. Thank God, Jeremy had made sure the property taxes were paid by the modest life insurance my aunt left, or I would have come back to nothing.

Looking around the place, I wondered what she must think of me and the choices I'd made for myself. More than anything, I always wanted to make her proud, but the last words I remembered her saying were:

"I raised you better than this, Shannon."

I trudged upstairs to the second bedroom that used to be mine. Even though the house now belonged to me, it just didn't feel right sleeping in her room. Besides, my bedroom always comforted me as a child, and I could definitely use some comfort now.

Thanks to Marissa, there were fresh linens on the bed and towels in the bathroom. Besides Gray, she had been the only one with a key, and I sincerely doubted he would bother.

I smiled as I saw the candles and bath oils that surrounded the rim of the tub. Marissa had thought of everything. My plans for the rest of the evening would be soaking in a long, hot bubble bath, eating the lukewarm burger from Charlie's, and going to bed. Maybe later, if I wasn't too tired, I would head down to the basement and find the box with all my DVDs and lull myself to sleep with a movie. It felt so good to do things on my own terms again.

I turned on the faucet of the tub, poured in the bath oil, and then went into my bedroom to undress. As I came into the room, I saw the window had been left partially open, and figured Marissa had left it that way to air out the staleness of the house. I would have to remember to close the other windows to protect against the chill of the night and... anything else that might be out there.

I shook that thought away. This wasn't the time to start spooking myself, even though I had returned expecting trouble. I pulled aside the curtains, started to close the window, and paused. Outside, a sheriff's SUV had pulled away from the curb and was already heading down the street. I kept watch until it was completely out of my line of sight. It was too dark to see who had been inside the vehicle, but instinct gave me the answer. I shut the window and locked it, wondering not for the first time what I would say to my ex-husband when I finally saw him.

That next morning, I walked the nearly two miles back to Charlie's. When I got there, I didn't immediately go inside, but stood outside for ten minutes, building up enough courage to go inside. I needed a job—my parole officer had made that very clear. I didn't have any problem being a server because it was what I'd done for two years after graduating high school. What made me hesitate was the fact that this was a central location for the town of Gypsy Bay. All the locals made Charlie's their place to be, especially on the weekends. If people didn't know I was back in town, they would surely know after one day of me working here.

Dammit. Maybe it was a mistake coming here, and by here, I meant Gypsy Bay. I should've told Jeremy to turn around and drive to San Francisco. I always loved that city, and I could hide there. Or maybe I would head farther south to Los Angeles, where I could definitely get lost. Better yet, how about I just leave California altogether and go so far away, no one would know who I was or what I'd done? Vermont sounded like a beautiful place.

The sound of gravel crackling under tires broke into my thoughts, and I turned to see the sheriff's SUV pulling into Charlie's parking lot and right beside where I was standing. I braced myself as the tinted driver's window lowered, and Gray showed his handsome tanned face. He had on big aviator glasses, and I hated the disappointment I felt in not being able to see his eyes. It had been three years since we last saw each other, and the first time we were talking without a glass partition separating us.

"Everything all right, Shannon?"

"Yeah. I'm fine."

"What are you doing here?"

I didn't answer, not really understanding the question. Was I forbidden from walking around the town?

He frowned at my silence and then opened the door to

his vehicle and stepped out. As always, he instantly towered over me, but I wouldn't back down, even though his presence was enough to intimidate even an innocent man.

But I didn't like looking up at him and instead turned my attention to the road and cars driving by as other people continued with their lives, while my life seemed to be standing still.

"Did you get the keys to your aunt's house?"

"I moved in yesterday," I said. "Thank you for keeping an eye on it."

He nodded but didn't move away, and I got the sense there was more he wanted to say. There was so much more I wanted to say, too, but this wasn't the time. With the tension so thick between us, I didn't know when there would ever be a good time to talk about the past. I wanted desperately to leave it buried, but I knew Gray would always continue to look for answers.

He took off his sunglasses, and I could feel his eyes steady on me. "Listen, don't take this the wrong way, but if you're hungry—"

"Goodbye, Sheriff."

I did look up at him this time and relished my first look into that light brown gaze that used to hypnotize me. But Gray was literally playing the role of the white knight, which came so naturally to him, and I didn't want it. I silently begged him not to say one more word, and he finally stepped back, got into his car, and drove away. He did make it clear, however, that he was pissed. I had to step out of the way of gravel being kicked up by his tires as he peeled out of the parking lot.

"Hey, everything all right?"

I turned to see Marissa coming outside. She was wearing her apron and shielding her eyes against the afternoon sun. I looked back to the road just in time to see Gray's SUV turn a corner and disappear.

"I saw you and the sheriff talking, but I was in the middle of taking an order and couldn't come out to rescue you until now."

I changed the subject quickly. "Is the night manager here yet?"

Marissa smiled, recognizing what I was doing. "Yes, and he's ready to hire you already."

I gave my friend a knowing look, and Marissa sighed.

"I'll admit he was a little concerned. But the night shift needs help, and he's willing to give you a trial run. Will you come inside now?"

I nodded and started to follow Marissa. Just before I reached the entrance, I stopped and noticed the wall of trees behind the restaurant. I'd nearly forgotten about them, and just beyond was Widow Lake. At night, it would be dark. So dark. A perfect place to hide, yet see so much.

CHAPTER THREE

Gray was in a dark mood, and it had nothing to do with the fact that it was Saturday night and he was spending his evening breaking up bar fights. It had been nearly three weeks since he last saw Shannon standing outside Charlie's diner, and she'd looked at him as though she might commit a second murder in her life. He didn't mean to insult her or imply she was some charity case, but for some dumb reason, it hadn't occurred to him she'd been looking for a job.

For three weeks now, she'd been the newest server at Charlie's, and for three weeks, he'd avoided the place, even though the diner had been his favorite dinner spot. Living alone with no wife or children, Gray didn't see a need to constantly spend time in his kitchen when he could easily pay someone else to make his meals. Plus, with his irregular hours, there were times he'd leave work too exhausted to even think about standing over a boiling pot of water to make himself something resembling dinner. It was true that several of the single ladies of Gypsy Bay wanted to help him rectify that, but Gray had spent the last four years thwarting them off. He indulged in an occasional one-night stand, but ever since he heard Shannon was being released…

The radio in his vehicle crackled to life, and the sounds of dispatch came through. Another fucking bar fight. Gray nearly responded to the call, needing to blow off some more steam, but one of his deputies who was already in the area beat him to it. He sighed, thinking he should just take his ass home. Truthfully, his shift had ended long ago, but as usual, he wasn't too eager to go home. He glanced at his wristwatch. Screw it. Charlie's would be closing soon, and if she was there, all the better. This was his town, and he wasn't going to avoid any of its citizens, even if one of them was his ex-wife.

* * *

Six years ago…

Gray sat at a window booth alone inside Charlie's restaurant and checked his watch for the hundredth time since he'd arrived twenty minutes ago. Any other day, he'd brush off Cody's lateness with the fact that it was just Cody and that he loved people waiting on him. But today, Gray wasn't in a doting older brother mood. He had less than a half hour left on his lunch break, and he needed every minute of it to speak to his brother and get everything he needed to off his chest. Even more importantly, he didn't want to be late returning from lunch and relieving the other deputies.

He'd been a sheriff's deputy for Gypsy Bay for just over a month now, and he still wanted to make a good impression, not only on the sheriff but to his colleagues and the people of this town. The Spencer name had come to mean something —mainly money, so when Gray Spencer, the oldest of the two boys, returned from college and announced he was going to be a deputy, everyone was both shocked and confused. Yes, he had a nice little inheritance left in trust by his mother and father after they'd both passed in a car accident, but he didn't want to live off their gift. Something inside him wanted his own income, his own living. He'd loved law enforcement growing up and wished his dad had taken him to the sheriff's station more as a kid than to his many corporate businesses in San Francisco.

He loved every day of it, even though he was still getting the curious stares and jealous looks from some of his colleagues who knew he didn't *really* have to be there. But he was there, and he wasn't leaving.

He wished the same thing for Cody. He wanted his brother to find something he loved other than women and parties. He wanted him to choose a career that was completely his own and make his own living outside of their parents' wealth. Their parents had left Gray the bulk of the estate, which included the businesses, the investments, and the house in Gypsy Bay's more affluent neighborhood, but Stephen and Sonya Spencer were no fools. They knew their youngest boy had more expensive tastes, so they left him a modest inheritance that would pay him a monthly stipend of twenty thousand dollars for the rest of his life. It was enough to live comfortably even in San Francisco, but Cody Spencer didn't want to live just comfortably. He loved playing the role of the rich kid, and he played it to the hilt with his fancy loft in San Francisco, expensive custom car, and anything else of material value he could cram into his life.

Gray was happy his brother was enjoying himself, but he didn't like that he was living beyond his means. He especially didn't like that at the end of each month, he received a call from the trust fund manager complaining that Cody had been to his office again, demanding that he release more money to him or give him an advance on next month's stipend. This time, however, the demands had turned to threats of violence. Gray had managed to calm the man down enough not to call the police and promised to speak to Cody. That was what this meeting was about.

He was going to demand, once and for all, that Cody either go back to school or get a job so he could support himself financially. His parents had raised Gray to look after his brother, but it was getting very tiring trying to babysit a grown man.

He checked his watch again. "Dammit, Cody," he muttered to himself and looked out the window to see if he could spot his car pulling into the lot.

"More coffee, Gray?"

He turned quickly and looked up to see Shannon Hollis standing beside his booth, holding a coffee pot. She had a pretty smile, deep and dark expressional eyes he could get lost in and beautiful brown skin the color of hot chocolate. He always looked forward to seeing her when he came into Charlie's, but she hardly ever looked at him or paid him any attention except to take his order or refill his drink. In fact, the only time she ever really acknowledged him was when he was here, but that was because it was her job. When he'd see her around town, she'd look at him and then look away quickly and run off. Either she was afraid of him, or she couldn't stand the sight of him, and he knew it wasn't the former. Shannon Hollis grew up with her aunt after she'd lost her parents at a young age. The two of them lived on a limited income in a modest home on Talley Street, but Shannon always kept her head held high, not letting it bother her one bit that she didn't have much. She seemed brave, determined, and definitely not afraid.

So it had to be him—the rich, white boy with his white privilege who had no business in her league, and that agitated him even more.

She was looking at him expectantly, and he realized he'd forgotten what she'd asked.

"Excuse me?"

She smiled again, this time cocking her head to one side. "I asked if you wanted more coffee."

He pushed his mug to the edge of the table, signaling he did want more and then turned to look out the window just in time to see Cody pull up.

"It's about damn time," he muttered.

"Anything else, Gray?"

He turned back to her. "No, and it's Deputy Spencer."

The look she gave him, as though he'd just kicked a two-week-old puppy, made him wish he could take that back. Why did he say that? Why was he so annoyed at this beautiful woman? Could it be that she'd smiled at him twice now, and he knew that was as far as it would go between them?

"I'm sorry," she said in a low voice before hurrying off, and he felt even more like the lowest piece of shit.

Cody walked up just in time to see Shannon run off. He whistled. "Whoa, what did I miss here?" he asked, sliding into the booth opposite Gray.

"You're late."

"Am I?"

Gray's jaw tightened. "I'm going to make this quick since you don't care about wasting my time."

"What the hell has gotten into you?" Cody said, signaling one of the servers to bring him a coffee.

"Mike called me today and told me how you went ape-shit in his office because he wouldn't give you any more money."

Cody chuckled. "That's a bit exaggerated."

Gray ignored Shannon as she walked up to fill Cody's coffee mug. He didn't want to see that wounded look in her eyes again. She'd be all right as soon as Cody worked his charm.

"Cream, sugar?" she asked.

Cody nodded and winked at her.

Gray's ego couldn't resist, and he looked up just in time to see a blush creep through her brown complexion. There, she was all right now, and it pissed him off even more.

After she left them, Cody stirred in his cream and sugar slowly and then sat back and eyed Gray. "Listen, I wouldn't have to bother Mike every month if the two of you agreed to up the amount I get. I gave him a budget like a good little boy, and he still refuses."

"Because your budget includes a bunch of crap you don't need. Clubs, drinks, prostitutes. Jesus, Cody, how old are you?"

Gray watched as his brother's eyes chilled, but he ignored it. Too many people, including him and his parents, had given in to Cody all his life, and as a result, they'd all created a monster.

"You wouldn't need any additional money if you had your own income."

Cody groaned. "Here we go again."

"I mean it. I had to convince Mike not to call the cops."

"The cops? For what? I never touched him."

"You threatened to rip his balls off."

Cody stared at his brother and then started laughing. "I'm sorry. I'm sorry. You'd be laughing too if you'd seen the old man's face when I said that."

Gray wasn't going to admit he had laughed a little when Mike called and repeated those words to him. He and Cody had grown up knowing Mike as one of their father's good friends, and he hadn't even so much as uttered a curse word, let alone used the word *balls*.

"All right, you had your fun. Call him and apologize."

Cody wiped tears of laughter from his eyes. "Will do, but that doesn't solve the problem that I'm low on cash." He leaned forward in his seat. "Listen, I understand the reason Mom and Dad left you the bulk of the estate. You were always better with money than I was."

Gray sighed, knowing his brother would never forget the day the contents of the will was read, and they both realized what their parents had done. Yes, it made perfect financial sense, but Gray wished his parents had discussed their decision with Cody and him before their death. Instead, they entrusted Mike to explain their reasoning behind Cody's limited inheritance, and as a result, it had created a rift between Gray and Cody that had never mended.

Who was he kidding? There had always been sibling rivalry between them, even while growing up. In Gray's experience, their parents had loved and supported both of their sons, but Cody would argue differently, insisting that Gray was always the favored one, and what he considered to be a pitiful monthly allowance his parents left him only furthered his suspicions.

"You don't always have to follow their wishes," Cody said. "They're not here anymore to dispute anything, and Mike is our attorney now."

Gray downed the last of his coffee and started to stand. "He's the executor of the estate. Mom and Dad trusted him to follow out their orders. No more advances, Cody. Get a job."

Cody reached out and grabbed for his shirtsleeve. Gray noticed a new look of desperation in his eyes. "Give me a break. You honestly expect me to go out and get a nine to five like you?" He eyed Gray's uniform with disgust. "What are you doing anyway? You got something to prove?"

Gray tore his arm away and stood. "Either go back and finish school or get a job. Either way, I gave Mike specific instructions not to give you any more than what the will states."

"What if I don't?"

Gray stared at his brother and got instantly sad. He didn't want it to come to this. "Or I'm going to do what I was instructed to do. I can lower your stipend by one thousand dollars anytime I want until there's nothing."

Cody stood and pointed a finger in Gray's face. "You do that, and I swear to God, I'll kill you, Gray! Who the hell do you think you are? You think because you've got some fucking badge you can boss me around too? Guess what, big brother, you're nothing but a joke around here. The rich kid playing cops and robbers. Go fuck yourself!"

The restaurant had grown completely quiet by now, but Cody simply gave his brother one last murderous stare, turned, and marched out, slamming open the doors and startling the patrons who were coming in.

Gray eyed his brother as he got into his car and drove away. He didn't realize he'd been clenching his fists the entire time Cody had been in his face. He wanted so badly to go a couple rounds with his little brother but didn't want to cause any more of a scene than they already had. He flexed his fingers, grabbed for his jacket, and peeled some money from his wallet. Conversation in the restaurant had resumed, albeit quietly, so Gray took his exit. But as he stepped away from the table, he didn't see the small form behind him, and as such, he slammed right into her, and two glasses of pink lemonade were now all over his uniform.

Shannon gasped, looked up at him, and nearly wilted from his look. He had to be wearing every imaginable range of anger on his face. Everything he felt from his parents leaving him to deal with his brother, Cody being spoiled rotten, the thought that his brother might be telling the truth and this town thought he was just playing deputy, to the realization that a smile inside Charlie's was all he would get from Shannon Hollis, probably showed on his face.

"I'm so sorry, Deputy. I'm so, so sorry." She immediately pulled a white hand towel from the back of her apron and began blotting his shirt front.

Her hands were touching him, he thought to himself, and they were getting lower and lower, making him...

He snatched the towel from her hands, blotted at the mess himself, and then threw it down onto the table. With that, he stalked out of Charlie's, knowing he was already late returning to work.

CHAPTER FOUR

When Charlie's closed up for the night, I waited around until everyone but the manager had left. I pretended to be waiting for a ride, but when he finally made his way to the office in the back of the restaurant to complete his nightly paperwork, I walked out into the chilly dark night alone. Aunt Christine's house was about two miles from Charlie's, which made it very convenient to ride my bike to work those days before she died. But I had outgrown and sold that bike a long time ago, so it would be just me and my legs tonight. It was Marissa's night off, and I told her the lie that I would get a ride from one of the other girls when I had no intention of doing so. It was why I waited for the others to leave. I didn't want the offers; I just wanted to be alone. Alone and seemingly vulnerable to whoever might be watching.

I took a deep breath and began my trek across the deserted parking lot but didn't make it more than several feet before a sheriff's SUV pulled into the lot and stopped right beside me.

Here we go again, I thought to myself.

The engine shut off, and Gray stepped out, rounded the truck and came to stand directly in front of me. I wished he hadn't come here because I wasn't ready to face him again. I didn't know what I had expected from him on our first encounter, but it was definitely not to be called a beggar.

"Where's your ride?" he asked, looking around the darkened lot.

"I don't have one, and before you say anything else, you know I don't live far from here."

"Far enough."

His dark gaze swept over me one last time before he turned and opened the passenger door. "Get in."

The way he stood there, I could tell he was braced for an argument, but I decided to surprise him, and without a word, climbed into the SUV and shut the door.

* * *

They both kept their attention forward, watching as the darkened road became illuminated by his headlights. He wanted to turn and look at her, believing her facial expression would give him some clue to her thoughts. Then he wondered why he even cared. He wanted one thing from Shannon Hollis, and that was a motive.

He'd expected her to raise hell the moment he said he was taking her home. He just knew she was about to let out a slew of creative language, but to his surprise, she simply got into the truck, giving him a sneak peek of her ass in those jeans.

When he woke from that coma and was told his wife had gone to prison for the murder of his brother, he remembered praying to God to keep her safe. He'd been afraid for her, not just for her safety, but for the innocence she would lose. It would change her. It had changed her.

That innocence was gone, replaced with anger and cynicism, all under the guise of a fully-grown woman. She'd kept fit but didn't appear skinny or undernourished. In fact, she seemed to have filled out more in these four years in places a man of his age could appreciate. She'd let her hair grow and allowed it to curl to its natural state, which made her look as if she'd just rolled out of bed.

Christ.

"It's the next turn on your right."

They both knew he knew where her Aunt Christine's house was. He supposed she needed a way to fill the silence by giving him directions, which had basically been the extent of their conversation since the moment he pulled away from Charlie's.

"How is your aunt's place working out for you?"

"It needs some work, but it's sturdy."

"It's a good thing the house isn't too far from the restaurant," he ventured.

"That's the idea," Shannon said. "When Marissa isn't working, I can easily walk home."

He frowned. "Is that what you've been doing for these past few weeks—walking home at nearly midnight?"

She kept her eyes straight ahead, which was answer enough for him.

"Look," he said, his jaw tightening, "It's my job to make sure the people are safe."

"Well, you can tell them all to stop hiding under their beds. Little Shannon got her homicide fix a long time ago."

"Jesus, Shannon, I meant you."

She laughed. "So you're telling me everyone is letting the past rest?"

A moment passed, and he said in a low voice. "They're trying to."

She eyed him hard. "Even you?"

He wasn't going down this road with her now, so he ignored that question and continued. "I'll have one of my deputies swing by and give you a lift when Marissa isn't there. If I'm available, I'll—"

"I don't need your help."

Gray turned to look at her and was met with anger and pain.

"I'll have Aunt Christine's old Toyota out of the shop soon, so you can stop trying to protect me," she said. "If you want to protect someone, start with yourself."

"What the hell is that supposed to mean?"

When she didn't answer him, he jerked the wheel to the right, and the SUV lurched to the side of the road. Before it came to a full stop, Shannon unbuckled her seatbelt and leaped out. Gray put the car in park and got out after her. It took him only two strides to catch up to her, grab her arm, and turn her toward him.

"Why are you here?" he asked, his face inches from hers.

"Because this is my home," she spat, yanking her arm free.

"Bullshit! What are you trying to do, show people that you've paid your debts? That even you can change?"

"I don't care what people think of me. I know what I did, and I know exactly what kind of woman I am."

She leaned in closer, and he could all but feel the whisper of her lips. "But you know what, Sheriff? I also know what kind of man Cody was."

He gripped both of her arms and shook her. "Don't! Don't you ever say his name. Every weekend for that first year, I came to see you, begging you to give me a damn motive. I needed you to give me one good fucking reason why you shot him. Anything to help me understand. But all you ever said was—"

"You don't want to understand this."

She said it in that same matter-of-fact way that made him

want to strangle her. He dropped his arms and stepped away from her.

"Good night."

It was then he noticed they were only two doors away from the house.

Shannon pulled her purse strap up to her shoulder and dug her hands into her coat pockets. "Thanks for the ride."

He didn't say anything, too angry and too exhausted to deal with her any more tonight. But she continued to stand there, staring at him now, as if she expected something from him. Then she was moving toward him so fast it caught him off guard. Ironically, had it been anyone else, he would have grabbed for his weapon, but Shannon, the town's femme fatale, kept him rooted to the ground as she stepped up to him, wrapped her arms around his neck, and kissed him.

* * *

Need. It was the only word to describe the reason I walked up to him and put my lips against his. Pure need. At that very moment, I needed him close to me. Despite my anger and frustration, I needed Gray close to me.

I could feel him restraining himself but not altogether pulling away. He was probably more shocked than I was, but as the moment intensified, something broke free, and he deepened the kiss, plunging his tongue into my mouth, wrapping his arms around my waist and tightening them.

I allowed myself these precious seconds of bliss and took full advantage by touching anywhere my hands could reach —his shoulders, neck, face. *Jesus, it's been too long, but this isn't why I came back.* I wasn't supposed to be indulging in midnight kisses with my ex-husband, reliving six-year-old memories and wishing...

Gray broke the kiss, backed away from me, and instantly,

I felt abandoned and lost, as we both stood there breathing hard while he stared at me as if he didn't know what to do with me.

With nothing more to say, I turned and hurried to my house. I didn't look back to see if he was still there but let myself inside, closed the door, and leaned my head back against the oak frame. I softly pounded the back of my head against it several times, wondering what the hell I'd been thinking.

That's when I smelled it. The faint scent of paint wafted its way to my nose. I removed my coat to fling it across the back of an armchair in the living room. I bypassed the kitchen in favor of heading upstairs to the bedroom. All I wanted to do was take a shower, watch an old movie, and fall asleep, only to get up, get ready for work, and repeat the day over again.

I didn't complain, however, in the least. In the weeks since my release, I'd come to look forward to those eight to ten hours working at Charlie's, and even took on extra shifts when they were available. Most of the women there were new to Gypsy Bay, and either didn't know about my past or didn't care. Maybe it was because they all looked as though they were carrying secrets of their own and didn't see any sense in judging me. They welcomed me from the moment I was hired as part of the family and even ran interference for me when any customers got too bold and tried to bring up that night four years ago. Yes, I could take care of myself; I'd learned how to do that real quick in prison, but it was nice knowing that others looked out for me too.

However, it bothered me very much when Gray Spencer tried taking care of me. It spoke to his basic decency and kindness that he still saw me as a human being and wanted to make sure I was safe. But I didn't deserve it in the least—not from him.

I pulled off one sneaker at a time and carried them upstairs, where the paint smell grew stronger. I wrinkled my nose to the strong stench, making my way along the corridor and into the master bedroom, which, after weeks, I'd finally decided to call my own. I stepped inside, felt along the wall for the light switch, turned it on, and then immediately wished I hadn't.

Red paint was smeared all along the walls, surrounding me, mocking me with its ugly script. Amid all of it was a picture of Cody, smiling in that charming and carefree way I remembered, taped to the center of the wall above my bed. I marched over, ripped it away and tore it in half. But, I couldn't get rid of the message that assailed me. Even if I shut my eyes to it, I could still see the angry red-painted scrawl all too clearly.

Murderer.

CHAPTER FIVE

The rhythmic sound of the hammer against nail seemed to calm Gray's nerves, which, ever since last night, ever since that kiss, had been on edge. He should have stopped that kiss the moment he sensed what she'd been about to do. But the truth was, he hadn't wanted to. It had been a long time since they touched each other. When he visited her in Chowchilla, they only stared at each other through a partition, and those visits weren't in the least bit romantic since he was only up there to grill her about Cody. But damn, that kiss opened up something inside him that had been buried deep, and now he couldn't stop thinking about it or her. He wanted more.

You're not getting any more, he thought to himself as he hammered another nail into wood. He needed to stay away from her. That was the pact he'd made with himself as soon as he found out she was getting early parole, and for his own sanity, he needed to remember that.

It was Saturday, his official day off, and he'd gotten up early from a restless sleep to drive down to the lake house and work on what was turning out to be a nearly four-year project. He'd bought the old place, which sat just off Widow Lake, for Shannon as a wedding gift, had it demoed, and even hired a contractor to get started on gutting it and getting it remodeled into the home she'd always wanted. Several times, on his days off, he would drop by and help with the construction. Working with the men and turning something old and ugly into something new and beautiful had turned out to be very therapeutic for him. Then something happened, and his mind refused to tell him. When he awoke from his coma, found out Cody was presumed dead, and his wife in prison for his murder, he fired the contractor and his crew and was content to let the place go into further ruin.

He started seeing Dr. Brian Kessler, one of Gypsy Bay's best psychologists, who specialized in memory recovery. Gray did sessions with him every week for nearly three months, reliving everything he could recall about the night of the crash. He looked into meditation, hypnosis, and even returned to the scene of the accident in the hopes he could get his mind to wake up.

When Dr. Kessler suggested that it was possible his mind didn't want to remember in order to protect him from the truth, Gray canceled his sessions and used his skills as a cop to try solving the case himself. But after weeks of reviewing case notes, interviewing the only witness, Mrs. Wicker, who'd only heard gunshots that night, and getting the silent treatment from Shannon each time he visited her, he gave up and returned to this old house.

He picked one room at a time and focused on one task and did his best to not focus on Shannon, Cody, and everything in between. Most times, he would have his iPod playing in the background. But on days when he chose to work in silence, his mind gave way to memories he thought he'd buried long ago.

"I'm going to buy it one day for Aunt Christine and me,"

Shannon said, her voice so young and excited. "It's been up for sale for two years now. Nobody wants this rundown thing."

"Why do you want this rundown thing?" he asked, watching as her face got animated.

"Because underneath all that"—she waved her hand indicating the dilapidated roof, the cracked and peeling paint, and the overgrown land as a whole—"I know she sparkles."

Gray picked up one of the many pieces of plaster that had fallen from the ceiling and snorted. "Yeah, she sparkles all right."

A car horn beeped twice outside, signaling someone coming up the circular driveway. Gray stepped over the debris that had been there since he'd had the place demoed and into the foyer. The front door was wide open to let out the musty smell of the old place, and he stood there in the entryway and watched as Jeremy Barrett got out of his car.

"I went by your office first," he said, by way of greeting. "When your secretary told me you were actually using your day off as a day off, something told me to check for you here."

Gray leaned against the doorframe and crossed his arms. "Am I that predictable?"

Jeremy shrugged. "Shannon's back in town. Must have triggered a lot of memories for you. Some of those having to do with this old piece of crap." He paused to look around and then shook his head. "I thought for sure you would have sold it after she left."

"You mean after she was sent to prison for manslaughter."

Jeremy's eyes narrowed, but he didn't say anything to that.

"Did you drive all the way out here to make an offer on this place or did you want to talk to me about something?"

"I want you to leave Shannon alone."

Gray said nothing, turned to head back into the living area and picked up his hammer to resume his work.

"I mean it, Sheriff," Jeremy's voice boomed loud and clear over the hammering.

"Who made you her protector?"

"Her aunt."

Gray paused, turned around, and eyed Jeremy with a questioning look.

"Yeah," he said. "Just before she died, she asked me to look after Shannon. She doesn't seem to want my help, but I'm keeping to my word. I'm all she's got now, and I can look out for her from a distance if I have to."

Jealousy ran all through Gray and seemed to settle somewhere in his spine. He wondered why Shannon's aunt never asked him to look after her since they had begun dating before her death. The time between their courtship and engagement had been almost nonexistent, but that was Gray's fault. He'd had her, and he didn't want to let her go, fool that he'd been. Still, by the time they were married, Christine had passed, and he never got a chance to earn the older woman's trust and respect.

He turned away from Jeremy, hammered once and then twice. "You think I'm a threat to her?"

"You tell me."

Gray gave a short, scornful laugh, bent down to pick up another nail, and started hammering again.

Jeremy continued. "Look, I can't be any clearer than this. There's too much conflict between you two. Considering the reason she was sent away in the first place, you can't blame me for being worried about her well-being in this town."

Gray hammered the nail one last time with so much force that he broke through the plaster. He tossed the hammer into the toolbox with a loud clang and whirled around to the lawyer turned Superman for Shannon.

"What the hell does she expect? Did she honestly think I'd be able to continue with my life knowing the answer to my brother's death lives only a few miles away?"

"I can't speak for her. All I know is that she loves Gypsy Bay. She has ever since she came to live here when her parents died. Now that Christine has passed, she can go anywhere she wants. I just don't think she wants to."

Gray's ego had him hoping her love for the town wasn't the only reason she wanted to stay, but he mentally kicked himself, remembering who this woman was. He needed to forget about the way she laughed, how damn sexy she was when she was being shy around him, how good she'd felt in his arms when they'd made love for the first time, how he'd felt like a million dollars when she said yes to being his wife. Guys like Cody who were handsome and charming usually got the confident, sexy, knockout beautiful girls. But this confident, sexy, knockout beautiful girl had wanted Gray. At least that was what he thought all those years ago.

"I'm not going to hurt her, and neither is anyone else. You can go tell her that. And while we're into passing messages back and forth like this is high school, you tell her I'll leave her alone when she tells me why she killed Cody."

"You know she didn't send me here, Gray," Jeremy said, lowering his voice. "She'd skin me alive if she knew I came to see you."

"Fine. Now get out."

Jeremy regarded him with what looked like a mixture of anger and sympathy. He took another look around the house, ending at the lake view beyond, and then sighed.

"Does she know you still have this place?"

Gray gestured to the parked car outside. "I have a lot of work to do."

"All right. All right." He raised his hands and backed away toward the foyer. "Listen, I know you want to know about your brother. Anybody in your situation would. But say you get the answers you want? What happens then?"

Gray took a deep breath and expelled it in frustration. "Please, don't stand there and tell me it's not going to bring Cody back because I already know that."

"I mean, what happens to her? To the two of you?"

Gray hated the fact that the man had been reading his thoughts. He hated that most nights he fantasized about Shannon coming home to him and the two of them picking up where they left off before their marriage had been infected by lies and murder.

Gray shrugged his shoulders. "Nothing. You said it yourself. You're all she's got now."

*S*ix years ago…

"He hates me," I said, staring out into the rain-soaked streets and looking across the road at the sheriff's station.

Deputy Gray Spencer—I wouldn't forget that title again—was inside, working late as always. Damn, he worked hard. Yes, he was the town's "rich kid," but he chose to find something of his own and not just simply live off his parents' money—unlike my companion sitting beside me.

Cody laughed. "I guarantee he doesn't hate you."

"Okay, maybe *hate* is a strong word, but I'm definitely not his favorite person right now."

"Jesus, Shannon, when did you ever start doubting yourself? You're a beautiful girl. You just need to up your charm a little."

"Isn't he seeing someone?" I asked, turning to face Cody.

He frowned. "You're stalling. Why?"

"Because I don't understand what we're doing here," I said, trying to keep the nervousness from my voice. "Your brother doesn't seem like the type who likes to play games."

"You think I'm playing games?"

I stared at him hard as a feeling of uneasiness rose in the pit of my stomach. "You're not playing matchmaker out of the goodness of your heart, Cody. What's in it for you if Gray and I are together?"

"I just want my brother to be happy. Is that so wrong? He's been acting like a prick lately, and I think if he just found a good woman to keep by his side, his mood would lighten."

I stared ahead and nodded slowly. "And Gray in a better mood might mean he'd part with more of his inheritance."

"Yeah, well, that would be a plus," he admitted.

I shrugged. "That's between the two of you. Don't hold me responsible if you don't get what you want."

"I wouldn't dream of it," he said, giving me that dimpled smile that made every woman in northern California sigh with bliss.

He nodded back toward the sheriff's office. "His shift ended an hour ago, but Gray never goes home when he's supposed to because there's nothing to go home to." He paused and looked at me. "You're going to change that. I want you to go up there, pretend you just walked from Charlie's restaurant, and that your friend couldn't come pick you up. Seeing you drenched from the rain and looking like the damsel in distress, it won't take him two seconds to offer you a ride home."

Cody looked out at the sheriff's station, watching his brother, and I knew I couldn't have imagined the look of subtle admiration in his eyes.

He cleared his throat. "Gray is one of the good guys."

I hesitated for a moment longer, thinking that, at this moment, I was hitting a fork in the road, and it might be safer to go right instead of left. But going right meant staying at Charlie's and just barely staying afloat with both my bills and Aunt Christine's care. I didn't like the fact that I was actually fishing for a husband, and even more stupid, I was fishing for a husband who was completely out of my pond. Gray Spencer was rich, young, handsome and white. Surely, he had his pick of women in the socialite circles of his parents. I remembered years ago, walking home on a Friday afternoon, and I'd seen the black town car pass down the road. Inside were Gray, Cody, and their parents, on their way to San Francisco for what would most likely be a beautiful gala or an event supporting the arts, orphans, the homeless, or some other noble cause. I remembered wondering how it would feel to experience that kind of life and chalked it up to nothing but a wishful fantasy.

However, after their parents had died, Cody continued to be a socialite but chose the hottest nightclubs in the city instead. Gray, being the enigma he was, had traded it all in for a deputy's badge.

"I'll be honest with you," Cody said. "I do need money, and it seems you and I both have that in common."

"There are other women out there who wouldn't mind dating Gray and would gladly go along with your plans," I argued.

"True, but have you ever asked yourself why I never stopped coming to you?"

He left the rest unsaid. When Cody came into Charlie's three months ago, looking handsome in his white shirt, brand-name fitted jeans, and loafers with his chestnut-colored hair and eyes to match, he'd made sure to sit in my section and monopolize my time. When he'd first suggested that I get his brother to marry me, I hadn't laughed but just stared. It was such an odd thing to suggest because the thought had never crossed my mind as being remotely possible. He'd said Gray and I would be good together, but I'd caught the whiff of his bullshit. When Cody had finally told me what he was really after, I'd given him the check for his coffee and sent him on his way.

But he'd come back the next day, and he kept coming back. With each refusal, Cody had persisted, and the medical bills continued to pile up, and the number of hours I worked couldn't catch up. I had been so filled with hopelessness and desperation that after three months, I surprised Cody by agreeing to his plan.

Gray Spencer was our solution, and we were both about to use him for our own personal gains. I thought about my aunt, and how I wished I could do more for her, but I'd halted my college education halfway through and come home to care for her. That left me with just enough work experience to be a server at Charlie's. It had been two years now, and Aunt Christine needed chemo and more than likely radiology treatments later on. Yesterday, she'd talked about using the equity in the house to pay for her care, but she owned it free and clear, and the last thing I wanted was for her to go into any more debt at her age. I needed Gray. I needed his money, and Cody was going to help me make that happen. Now, if only I could get my conscience to shut up, this would be easy.

I made a big show of doubting myself in front of Cody, but what I didn't tell him was that deep inside, I knew Gray liked me. I could see it for just an instant whenever he looked my way before he masked it again. I would find a way to work on that. Maybe I wasn't in love with him, but I admired and respected him a lot, and for now, that would have to be enough.

I reached for the door handle of the car and opened it, and the sound of rainwater instantly filled the silence.

"Remember this, Shannon," Cody said, raising his voice above the pelting drops. "My brother has two weaknesses, and one of them is trusting people too much."

I paused, one foot out of the car, and turned to look back. "What's the other?"

His smile turned wicked. "You."

I didn't say anything to that but got out of the car, put the hood of my jacket up, and walked briskly toward the sheriff's station. As I neared the bright lights dancing inside, I could see Gray hunched over his desk, his complete focus on the computer screen. I turned back to Cody just in time to see him drive away.

It wasn't until then that I responded to his last words. "I know."

CHAPTER SEVEN

I was folding silverware into cloth napkins when the familiar chime of Charlie's bell rang. Since the last of the lunch crowd had left an hour ago, it had slowed down considerably. Now, with tables cleaned and tip money collected, I forced myself to do busy work until the dinner crowd started coming through.

I looked up expectantly from a booth in the back corner of the restaurant, grateful to see a customer. Then I saw it was Gray who came through the door and inside. Something old and familiar stirred, as it always did.

That night I found the word "Murderer" on my wall, I ran back outside, yelling Gray's name, but he'd already left, and I never said a word about it to anyone. Maybe that was foolish, maybe not, but I knew I didn't want him, Marissa, or Jeremy to become alarmed. So instead, I chalked it up to some mischievous teenagers who somehow got access to my home while I was away. I slept on the couch in the living room with all my doors and windows locked, and the next morning, I went to the hardware store, bought new door and window locks, a gallon of primer, and some crème butter paint. Yes, it was vandalism, but reporting it would bring the deputies to the house, and deputies led to Gray.

Painting the bedroom had helped to calm my nerves, and the resulting new color made me feel for the first time hopeful about my new life. If I was going to stay in Gypsy Bay, I might as well fix up my aunt's old house and make it my own.

Then the thought of renovating brought back memories of the house Gray had bought me, the one we were supposed to fix up together. God, I'd loved that house. From its broken-down roof to its termite-infested basement. No doubt, he'd sold it and everything else that reminded him of me. I promised myself I'd visit the house and see if the new owners had made any improvements. I was free to do so now that I'd taken Aunt Christine's old Toyota in for a tune-up. The car had sat idle in the carport for nearly five years. On my second day in Gypsy Bay, I went out to the side of the house and threw off the tarp to give the old car a once-over. I got inside, turned the ignition, and let out a happy yell when the engine came to life. Then, my gleeful mood crashed when the car abruptly shut off. I called Neil's Garage and had it towed, but I'd been unable to pick it up until I'd saved enough for the repairs. That day had finally come, and I could begin my work and the main reason I had returned to Gypsy Bay. The only problem was, my plans involved the sheriff, which meant it wasn't going to be easy.

I studied Gray as he sat down in a booth across from a female in a deputy's uniform. He had respected my wishes that night by staying away from me. For the past week, when he would see me around town, he'd give a curt nod and continue on as though I were any other citizen. That was fine with me because if Gray wasn't watching me, he wouldn't find out I was watching him.

Karen, one of the servers on the morning shift, came up

and sat down across from me in the booth. She turned to watch the sheriff and his companion and turned back to me with a wry smile.

"For someone who's trying to forget him, you sure do like to stare at him a lot."

I ignored the statement and asked, "Who's the pretty blonde in uniform?"

"The newest deputy, Leah Collins. She just moved from San Francisco with her two-year-old son. The sheriff has been training her."

I didn't say anything but continued rolling the silverware into the napkins, each movement deliberate and precise.

"You know they're in your section, right?"

I stopped, feeling my eyes grow wide. "What? Oh, God, trade me, please. I'll take the next one seated in your section."

"You really are out of it, aren't you? Look around, sweetie." Karen waved her arms about the restaurant. "This is the calm before the dinner rush. I'm clocked out, and the other girls haven't come in yet. You're it for the next half hour."

I sighed and stood from the booth. Karen rolled her eyes at me as I walked by. "I swear. Whenever he's not looking, you're looking at him. Whenever you're not looking, he's looking at you. Do you know how aggravating that is to watch?"

I ignored her and wiped my hands on the back of my jeans and approached the table as though it were full of vipers. When Gray saw me coming, he looked around as though he were ready to call for backup.

"Hello, Sheriff."

"Shannon," he returned with a simple nod.

I pointedly turned to Leah Collins, waiting for an introduction. Gray took the hint.

"Shannon, this is Deputy Leah Collins. She just joined our team a couple of weeks ago from San Francisco."

I forced a smile. "Why Gypsy Bay?"

Deputy Collins laughed. "Strange, isn't it? Actually, I was with the SFPD for ten years. Then I had my son and took a leave of absence. Then my husband lost his job, so we decided to move down here and move in with my mother-in-law."

"Your husband is here too?" I asked, trying not to look so relieved.

"He's still in San Francisco finalizing the sale of our house, but he'll be here in a few weeks. I needed to help bring in some income, so I joined the sheriff's department down here."

"It's nice to have you," I said, pulling out my notepad and pen and stealing a look at Gray.

"Thanks," she said, a big smile coming across her face. "That's nice to hear, considering I've been getting the 'city cop coming up here to intrude on our small town values' looks."

Gray chuckled. "It could be worse."

I looked at him, wondering if he really meant to say that. When he looked pointedly at me, I realized he did. He wasn't going to apologize for that, so I removed the wounded look from my face.

Deputy Collins must have sensed she had started some tension and rushed to fill in the silence. "Forgive me if I sound rude, but this is a small town compared to San Francisco, and rumors are flying about you. You're Shannon Hollis, right?"

"Whatever you heard, most of it is probably true," I said. "And it's still Spencer."

The deputy divided a look between Gray and me. "So the two of you are, or were..."

"Yes," we both said in unison.

"Right," was all Leah could say in reply.

"Right," I echoed.

I was done with the conversation, but before I could ask for their orders, Gray's radio came to life. "Sheriff, you need to get up to the ridge by the Oakwood trails as soon as possible."

Gray frowned and pulled his radio out. "What's the problem?"

"We found a body up here. Looks fresh."

"Well," Leah said, getting up from the booth. "Finally, some excitement. It was nice to meet you, Shannon."

"You too," I said, backing away from the booth as they both stood and quickly headed for the door.

After the two of them were gone, I continued to stand there, rooted to the ground and clutching the notepad in my hands as fear slowly coursed its way through me.

CHAPTER EIGHT

Gray and Leah were in his SUV, pulling away from Charlie's restaurant when she spoke up. "You miss her?"

Gray didn't bother playing coy and asking who she was talking about. "No."

"No disrespect intended, Sheriff, but you're lying."

He frowned, glanced at her, and then quickly looked away.

"It's all right if you do. You two were married for how long before it happened?"

Gray's gut clenched as he tried to push the memories back. "Just over a year."

"So you were newlyweds, blindly in love and passionate for each other."

He snorted. "Do you read a lot of romances, Deputy?"

"That kind of passion doesn't just go away."

"Are you her cheerleader now? She's a murderer."

"She was convicted of manslaughter. I read about the case. It interested me. No body. No motive." Then she added softly. "You were in a coma at the time, right? You didn't get a chance to see her before they took her away."

He didn't say anything, which she obviously took as a yes. "I'm sorry about your brother, and I'm sorry about the two of you and what it did to you."

"Thank you," he said, hoping that was the end of it.

"She kept her name," Leah said.

Gray snorted. "She was in prison. It wasn't like she could just go down to the courthouse and request a name change."

"Okay, so call me a romantic. You two look good together."

Gray didn't want to tell her they *were* good together. That is until the dream ended.

"You really should talk to her. If it helps in the least, she misses you too."

"How do you know that? Did you two have a slumber party or something?"

She pinned him with a look that told him to grow up. "Because the moment I told her I had a husband, her fists unclenched."

* * *

Gray was relieved to finally see the break in the road that led up to the wooded hiking trails. He didn't want to talk about Shannon or Cody anymore. For the past four years, he'd thrown himself into his work, intent on burying the past with Cody. Now, with Shannon's return, he often found himself not concentrating on the job at hand for thinking of her and the memories she brought back with her. Still, he was determined to keep his focus. He wasn't going to allow her to come back to his town and screw up everything he worked so hard for. People finally respected and admired him. They saw him as more than Stephen Spencer's son or

Cody Spencer's big brother. But the return of his ex-wife had already started the gossip tongues wagging. People wondered if he still had a soft spot for her and if that would interfere with his duties as sheriff of the town. It made him want to smash something because he couldn't outright deny either one.

He pulled the SUV to the side of the road along with several other sheriff's department vehicles, and he and Leah got out and made their way up the trail.

The body lay several yards ahead, blanketed among trees, wildflowers, and dead leaves. One male, approximately thirty-seven to forty years old was dressed in jeans, a light-weight jacket, and hiking boots, with three gunshot wounds to the chest. Gray assessed the body overall and looked around, addressing his deputies.

"Who found him?"

"A couple hiking on the trail," one of them replied. "They gave us their statement."

"They didn't hear any shots fired?" Gray asked.

The deputy shook his head. "That's the first thing I asked. They said they didn't hear anything. They were on this trail and nearly tripped over his body."

Gray looked at the dead man again. "Anybody know him?"

Everyone replied in the negative.

Gray frowned, looking around. "This area is pretty isolated, except for the main road just down there. How did he get up here? Any reports of abandoned cars come through lately?"

One of his deputies spoke up. "That's the thing, Sheriff. No ID and no car keys were found on him."

"There isn't a lot of blood either," Gray murmured.

"You think he was shot somewhere else and put here to be found?" Leah asked.

Gray didn't answer but kneeled down to get a closer look. He looked across the body and addressed the medical examiner who was still conducting his study. "What do you see?"

The man cleared his throat. "With the gunshot wounds to the chest, I'll need to do an autopsy to determine which bullet killed him. But it looks like he's been dead for nearly twenty-four hours. No defensive wounds from what I can tell."

The killer just walked up to the victim and shot him three times. Gray suddenly felt as though something was wrong. He looked up at his deputies and realized they were all regarding him with apprehension. He slowly stood and eyed them.

"Something I'm missing?"

They gave each other the briefest of looks, and then one of them stepped forward holding an evidence bag. "These were found clenched in his hands."

Gray looked into his eyes for any sign of clarity, but the young man just looked away. He took the bag, held it up, and suddenly realized why he'd been called to the scene of a routine murder that any of his people could have handled on their own. Inside the clear plastic bag were two items: a woman's diamond and ruby tennis bracelet and a small scrap of paper with the word *Murderer.*

Deputy Collins stepped forward to get a look at the evidence bag. She looked up at Gray and frowned. "Do you recognize it?"

He didn't say anything but kept eyeing the jewelry that he did indeed remember. He didn't even need to read the inscription to confirm it.

CHAPTER NINE

I sat in the basement of my house and peeled the tape off another box to rummage through it. It was my day off from the diner, and even though I didn't mind extra shifts, I was glad for the break. Marissa had been upset the manager didn't give us the same days off, but I was grateful. I loved my friend, but I'd never be able to accomplish what I needed to do if she was always around.

I was glad whoever packed my things had the foresight to label the boxes. It had saved me lots of time as I bypassed several containers and went through only those labeled *Miscellaneous*—at least, that's what I figured a gun would be categorized under. Aunt Christine purchased the gun years ago, deciding that two women living alone needed protection, and I wasn't very fond of dogs. As I searched, I worried that maybe Gray had seen it and purposely didn't include it with my belongings. It was a strict clause in my probation that I was not to carry a gun, and a sheriff would know that. But, hell, what was I supposed to do, sit back and wait idly for…

"Here you are," I said as I pulled out a small wooden box,

encasing the gun. I opened the lid, and there it was. My aunt never used it except to take me to the shooting range when I was younger. The barrel felt heavy in my hand, but as I gripped it and got used to its weight, I felt safe and empowered.

I started to close the box and noticed the hot pink velvet bag resting at the bottom. I picked it up, pulled open the drawstring, and took out the vibrator inside.

I did a mental happy dance.

I'd have to clean it first since it had obviously been in the box for at least three years. Then embarrassment colored my face as I thought about who in the world had packed my things and saw this. Did Gray hire someone or had he packed everything himself?

Jesus.

It wasn't like he'd never seen it before. I recalled the day after we returned from our honeymoon, and I was moving all of my meager belongings into his mansion on the quiet cul-de-sac. I'd labeled the small box *bedroom accessories* and was adamant that only I carry it. But the moment I entered the master bedroom suite and saw the large king-sized bed I'd be sharing with my husband, I had been shocked, dropped the box, and everything spilled out all over the floor. Gray, of course, had come up behind me just in time to see me stuffing the pink toy back inside. He knelt down beside me, stilled my hands, and brought it back out to examine it.

"Wow," was all he'd said.

I was mortified as I tried wrenching my hand free. I didn't know what type of women Gray had dated before me but could only picture Ivy League sorority types who didn't carry around pink, twelve-inch sex toys.

"I'll get rid of it," I'd said in a rush, piling the things back into the box and standing to rush out of the room.

"Shannon, wait," he'd called, but I ignored him, already

feeling like I'd just got a big black checkmark in the *Shannon is a crappy wife* column.

I smiled to myself, realizing how childishly I'd acted that day. Then I got warm inside, remembering how Gray had alleviated my embarrassment by making me feel alive and sexy.

I'd taken a day trip to San Francisco with Marissa where we'd had lunch and window shopped. When I returned that evening, Gray's sheriff's vehicle was in the driveway, and I was happy to see he wasn't working but figured he'd probably be in his office doing paperwork.

* * *

The house was dark when I entered, save for a lamp on the console table in the hall. I dropped my keys on it and saw a note scribbled in Gray's handwriting.

Come upstairs.

I frowned, clutched the paper in my hand, and made my way up the expansive curved stairs to the second level.

"Gray," I called out.

"In the bedroom," he answered.

I came to the open doorway and saw he was in the sitting area by the bay windows. Wearing a pair of jeans and no shirt, he had one leg crossed over the other knee. His hands were laced together, and he was the picture of contentment. I loved Gray's broad shoulders and arms, but part of him was cast in shadow. I moved nearer to him, wanting to get a better look, hoping to touch him.

"Stop," he said, halting my steps. "Take off your clothes, and get on the bed."

That gave me pause. This was the first time Gray had ordered me to do anything, and I was shocked by how much it turned me on. I backed up toward the bed and slowly reached for my top, taking it off and exposing the lace bra I wore underneath. Then, thinking he wanted a strip show, I slowly eased my jeans down past my butt.

"Hurry, Shannon," he said, and I heard the slight hitch in his breath.

Okay, so apparently he didn't want to be teased. I stepped out of my jeans and kicked them to the side, suddenly feeling awkward.

"Turn around, look on the bed, and tell me what you see."

I did, and when I looked at the bed, I realized with horror that he'd found my vibrator. I lied when I said I'd get rid of it. In truth, I'd packed it away again in the same box and shoved it somewhere in the garage. He must have found it when he was cleaning it out to make room for my things.

"What do you see?"

I picked it up and turned back to face him. "It's my vibrator. Gray, listen, if you don't want me to have it—"

"Take off your panties."

"What?"

"Take. Off. Your. Panties." He said it slowly and deliberately, and still hadn't moved one muscle from that relaxed position he was in. He just sat there, studying me, but I couldn't read his face.

I pulled the matching blue panties down between my legs, stepped out of them, and clenched them in my hands.

He groaned. "Lie on the bed and let me see you play with it."

I was literally shocked into immobility. "Gray, no. I can't do that."

"Why not?"

"Because I…it's private."

"I'm your husband. I want to see you do it."

I wasn't sure what he was up to, but suddenly, my excitement was vanishing, and my defenses were rising. "If you're trying to punish me for bringing it into your house—"

He rose so quickly, and before I knew it, he was upon me, and I was being pushed onto the bed, with his body hovering over mine.

"First of all, this is *our* house. Second, I want you to feel me and tell me who's really punishing whom."

He grabbed for my hand and pressed it against the crotch of his jeans. The hardness I felt there was unmistakable, and it turned me on.

"Now, I want you to take this damned vibrator"—he took my other hand that held the toy into his own—"and let me watch you use it."

He used his thumb to flick the switch, turning it on, and both of our hands traveled down between my legs and teased at the folds of my pussy. I closed my eyes and moaned instantly.

"That's it," he said, "show me how you play with it."

I felt him ease away from me and off the bed, and then I opened my eyes in time to see him resume his seat by the window, once again covered partly in shadow. The scene was so erotic as I pictured it from a stranger's viewpoint, standing at the entry to the bedroom, watching my husband remain completely still in an armchair, while he watched me undulate and moan on the bed with a large object buried deep between my thighs.

"Take off your bra, baby."

With my free hand, I unsnapped the hooks and let the material fall to the side of the bed. Immediately, I began rubbing my tender breasts and teasing my aroused nipples, building the sensations higher and higher. I knew I was about to come, but if Gray wanted to see it all, I would show him all. I took a breath to keep my waiting orgasm at bay, turned over onto my stomach, and rose to my knees. With my ass out and pussy exposed to him, I turned and watched him over my shoulder as I buried the toy deeper.

"Dammit, Shannon," he hissed.

But as I watched him, feeling the ecstasy build, I wished for him to be inside me and filling me.

"Gray, please," I cried, on the verge of orgasm. "I need you."

That was all the encouragement he needed. I watched him rise from the chair and reach the bed in two strides. He pulled the vibrator out of me slowly, tossed it to the side, and unzipped his pants. The next thing I felt was him slamming into me, and I cried out in delight.

It didn't take long. We were both on the edge as he thrusted in and out of me, and I answered, throwing my ass back at him. In under a minute, we were coming, gasping, and holding onto each other, desperate to prolong the moment.

Later, as I lay cuddled against him with sleep nearly overpowering me, I felt his arms tighten around my waist as he whispered into my hair.

"Don't ever feel embarrassed around me again."

CHAPTER TEN

The morning after the body was discovered, Gray was sitting in Mayor Eric Porter's office. He knew it was inevitable—a murder happened in a town that hadn't experienced murder in the last four years, and everyone wanted answers. Gray understood completely; he just didn't like the fact that his murder investigation was about to get political.

"Who was the guy?" asked Mayor Porter, a tall, lean, and handsome African-American man and Gypsy Bay's youngest mayor to date. He was forty-six, and he aged well, leaving the town's female population breathless each time he was in public view.

Gray handed him a copy of the file he'd prepared just for this meeting. "We ID'd the victim as Frank Miles, visiting from San Francisco. He checked in at Riverview Lodge on Friday and was paid up until Monday. He was thirty-eight years old, single, no kids, and worked as a delivery driver."

"So, he was just here for the weekend to hike," the mayor confirmed.

Gray nodded. "This is the season."

Eric was rocking back and forth in his desk chair across from Gray. He looked to be studying the file, but when he looked up and pierced Gray with cool, coffee brown eyes, he realized the man had only been thinking and carefully weighing his words for his next question.

"Any suspects?"

Gray returned his stare and said simply, "Not at this time."

Eric chuckled and stood from his desk to begin slowly pacing across the large office.

"You and my wife are the only ones who know how to stare me down with the straightest faces, and can almost convince me you're not holding something back."

Gray turned in his chair to face the mayor. "I don't know what you want me to say, sir. It's too early in the investigation to determine a suspect."

A knock came at the closed door, and Eric commanded for whoever it was to come in. The door opened and Gray just knew his day was about to get worse.

Gretchen Miller, assistant prosecutor for Marin County, walked in like always, as though she demanded attention. She and Gray had gone to college together. After graduation, both returned to Gypsy Bay; he believed he could do good in a small town, whereas she was unable to secure a high-paying attorney job in one of San Francisco's elite law firms. She'd cut her dark, curly hair shorter but still wore the pencil skirts that showed off her curves, and high heels that made her legs go on forever. He couldn't deny she was an attractive and ambitious woman, but she danced between that delicate line of ambition and ruthlessness, which was why he couldn't see a future with her. The last time Gray had seen her was three months ago. She was leaving his bed at four thirty in the morning, heading to the airport for a business trip, and saying something about not wanting things to get weird between them. She'd always preferred the casual relation-ships, and after he and Shannon divorced, that suited him just fine. Now…he wasn't sure what suited him. He wasn't sure of much of anything these days.

Gray divided a look between the mayor, who someday wanted to run for governor of the state, and the ADA, who dreamed of crossing the lines and becoming a sought-after defense attorney. Yeah, this case had become political long before Frank Miles had been found on that hiking trail.

"Sheriff Spencer, I believe you've met ADA Miller."

Gray stood and extended a hand to Gretchen. "Good to see you again."

"You, too, Gray," she said, flashing a beautiful smile that didn't quite make it to her eyes. "You look good."

He nodded and offered her the seat next to him.

"We were just going over the recent murder of the hiker," Eric said, still standing and resuming his slow pacing. "The sheriff tells me he hasn't determined any suspects in this case yet."

Gretchen's smile lessened only a little before she turned back to the mayor. "Well, I've come to know the sheriff as very cautious. He likes to dot all his I's and cross his T's, which is admirable. But when you've got the evidence staring you boldly in the face—"

"What evidence?" Gray asked.

"The bracelet, of course."

"It doesn't make her a suspect."

She faced him again, wide-eyed with a hint of glee. "So you have considered her?"

"I assume we're talking about Shannon Spencer," Eric interjected.

Gray looked to him. "Mayor, I know she has a record, but I don't want to turn this investigation into a witch hunt. If we focus on one suspect too early, we run the risk of being wrong and giving the real culprit a chance to cover their tracks."

"I agree with you, Sheriff," Eric replied. "But does she have an alibi for that night?"

Gray took a deep breath, realizing he was losing ground. "No. Her manager told me it was her night off."

Eric studied him again, and this time Gray felt a little of the man's sympathy. He took his seat across from them and leaned forward. "Look, I know you two have a history, and I'm not trying to do your job, but if the bracelet belongs to her, she at least needs to be brought in for questioning."

Gray nodded and stood. "Yes, sir. Thank you for your time. I'll see you later, Gretchen."

Before he reached the door, Eric called his name. Gray turned to see two faces watching him apprehensively.

"I don't want to have to remove you from this case due to conflict of interest. If you can't handle it…" He trailed off, probably seeing the anger slowly flooding Gray's face.

Eric paused and then held his head up with renewed authority. "Bring me a suspect, then bring me a killer."

* * *

"Sheriff!"

Gray halted before getting inside his SUV and turned to see Gretchen rushing in her six-inch heels to catch up to him.

"Looks like we're going to be working together," she said.

He nodded. "Come by the office if you want to take a look at the crime scene photos."

"I'll do that," she said, hurrying to keep up with his long strides. "Tell me; what do you think of the bracelet?"

Everything inside him stiffened, and he was glad he'd put

on his aviator shades to disguise anything she might see in his eyes.

He shrugged. "It was left clutched in the man's hand along with a note."

"Murderer," she said. "I know, but why the bracelet? What does it mean?"

"We're still trying to figure all that out." He made a show of looking at his watch. "I've got to get back."

"But it is hers?"

"The inscription on the inside indicates it belongs to Shannon, but I still need to confirm this."

She looked away, grinning as if she knew he was holding back on her but wasn't going to pursue it at this time. Then she faced him again. "The Mayor likes you. He's going to give you the benefit of the doubt, but you need to remember he's just as ambitious as me. He's got lots of goals, and if this case goes the way I think it's going to go, it would be good for all of our careers."

"I like being sheriff."

She continued, ignoring his comment. "If I see you playing favorites in any way, I'll make sure you're booted off this case."

"I believe you."

She smiled and then cocked her head to one side and stepped closer to him. She put one hand up to his cheek and brought her lips close to his but didn't kiss him.

"Now that the ugly part is out of the way, I'd like to tell you how much I've missed you."

They stood there together for several moments before she stepped back, turned, and walked away.

"Call me sometime," she said over her shoulder. "This case would be so much more fun if we could add the personal side to it again."

CHAPTER ELEVEN

I was on my knees, re-sanding the porch swing and so caught up in my project and singing along to some of my old music that I hadn't heard the booted feet walking up behind me.

"Shannon."

I gasped, turned, and fell on my butt. "Gray, Jesus!"

"I called your name twice," he said, leaning down and offering his hand to me.

I looked at his hand, at him, and then his hand again, and finally allowed him to help me up. Immediately, I started dusting myself off and touching my hair, only to find that it was still in the messy top knot I'd styled this morning after getting out of the shower. No one ever came to visit me, except for Marissa and Jeremy, so I never bothered to make myself presentable. So why did I suddenly want to run in the house, change out of my sweats, brush my hair, and put on a little mascara?

"What can I do for you, Sheriff?"

"Can we talk inside?" he asked.

I wanted to say no but thought that would sound petty

and childish. Without a word, I opened the screen door and left him to follow me inside. I walked to one side of the living room and turned back to face him. He was such an imposing presence. He'd always had the ability to make me feel small and cornered, that if he got his hands on me, he'd consume me. I gave a small shiver, because years ago before everything happened, he would lift me up in his arms, crush me against him, and make me beg for him. I used to love being consumed by him.

"Have you heard about the body we found?"

I let out a breath. "Yes. All the girls at Charlie's won't stop talking about it. The customers are giving me strange looks, but no one has been rude enough to come right out and ask me if I shot the man." I paused. "Is that why you're here? To ask me if I did it?"

He ignored my question and pulled out a small plastic bag labeled *evidence* and handed it to me. My eyes looked past the scribbled note to the very familiar bracelet, and my heart sped up. I felt myself moving to the sofa, and without realizing, dropped down onto the cushions, still staring at the jewelry.

I shook my head in confusion but trusted myself enough to speak. "I thought I'd lost this."

"It's yours, then?"

I nodded, still remembering the day it was given to me. The white gold was a bit tarnished now, but the diamonds and rubies winked at me, mocking me.

I finally looked up to see him watching me carefully. "Where did you find it?"

"Clutched in the hiker's hands along with that note."

Murderer. I still hadn't told him about the break-in or the red-painted walls I'd found when he drove me home that night. I told Marissa, and she insisted I tell Gray, even threatened to tell him herself, but I promised her I'd tell him, only to keep her quiet. Even though it felt like the perfect time to tell him now, I kept my mouth shut and my emotions in check.

"I need you to go through your things," he said. "Check to see if anything is missing. I had everything boxed up and put into your cellar."

"Yes, I know. I went through some things already."

I couldn't help the stab of pain and grief. He'd packed my things and moved them out of his home as soon as I was taken away. I chuckled to myself, thinking of the old cliché of a scorned woman who threw her husband's things out onto the curb in trash bags. But in my reality, my husband had been the one scorned, and I had been the wife thrown out of my house. I couldn't blame him for it in the least. I just wished it didn't suck so much.

Gray reached into his pocket, pulled out a business card, and wrote something on the back before putting it on the coffee table.

"If you find anything missing, call me. My cell number is on the back."

"Am I a suspect?"

"No."

"A person of interest?"

He regarded me for a minute. "Where were you on May seventeenth around six-thirty in the evening?"

Watching you. "I was here."

"Alone?"

"Yes, alone."

He turned and headed for the door. "You should consider getting yourself some more friends, besides Marissa. Meet some of the girls you work with after shift or on your days off."

"Most people like to keep their distance from a convicted felon, Gray. Even you."

He whirled around and stomped toward me so fast, I backed up impulsively, stumbled, and nearly fell to the ground, but he held me up with both hands clutching my arms.

"Stop calling yourself that! If you're going to live here and make me go crazy each time I see you, you may as well start referring to yourself as one of us. And just so you know, I'm only staying away because you and that lawyer of yours asked me to."

He pulled me close and up against his body, and I felt every inch of him, hard and strong. He then skimmed his lips along the curve of my neck and up to the outer lobe of my ear.

"Have you changed your mind?"

I moaned, feeling myself grow moist. He was hard between my legs, and it had been too damn long since I'd felt a man—Gray—inside of me. I began to rub myself along his body like a cat in heat, silently begging for what I needed.

"What do you want?" he asked, moving his hands down to my ass and pulling me closer to his hardness.

"Gray, please," I begged.

He moved his lips over my skin, never quite touching but close enough that it was driving me mad. He finally stopped at my ear, gently bit and tugged at the flesh, and whispered so softly.

"Tell me what happened that night, Shannon."

I froze, and like a bucket of cold water had been thrown at me, my fantasy was washed away. I pushed away from him and stepped as far away as possible, trying to regain my composure.

"You need to leave."

He turned away from me, bent to pick up the evidence bag with the bracelet, and headed for the door.

I had my arms wrapped tightly around me as though to

protect myself from him and the way he made me feel. I suddenly felt humiliated and used and couldn't resist one last counterattack.

"You know, the last time I remember seeing that bracelet, it was five years ago, and you were putting it in your back pocket."

He turned and stared at me, his eyes narrowing.

I lifted my chin, hoping he could see I wasn't as rattled as I felt. "Along with the other jewelry Cody gave me."

CHAPTER TWELVE

*F*ive years ago…

I couldn't stay in the bathroom forever.

I'd gone in there, closed and locked the door, turned on the water to disguise my movements, and sat down on the edge of the tub. That was fifteen minutes ago.

I'd been so brave when I walked into the sheriff's office nearly ten months ago, so sure of myself when I convinced Gray he was the only man I wanted two months later, and completely self-confident when I agreed to his marriage proposal a month after that.

Now, here I was, nearly a year later, hiding inside a hotel bathroom, on my honeymoon, and completely scared out of my mind because, on the other side of that door, my new husband waited for me.

I rose from the edge of the tub and made my way to the sink and vanity where I splashed water on my face and patted it down with a towel. I kept the towel to my face and inhaled and exhaled into it deeply. Only then did I look at myself in the mirror.

"Coward," I muttered to my reflection.

The plan had sounded so intriguing, but now that it had seemed to work so well, it suddenly hit me that this was Gray Spencer—a man I respected. Hell, if I was really being honest with myself, I'd admit to finding him very attractive in that brooding way of his. And I wasn't alone in my feelings. Most of the women of Gypsy Bay shared my opinion, and I'd gotten many envious looks when it was known I would become Mrs. Spencer.

Then came the whispers. A young black waitress marries the heir of one of the wealthiest white families in northern California. The only thing missing from this cliché was a baby. I did my best to ignore all the names being tossed at my back: gold digger, opportunist, in the family way, even blackmailer. It was ironic, because none of those names suited me but one, and it was just as ugly.

Liar.

The rumors and gossiping didn't bother me. It was when the talk got back to Aunt Christine that I finally had to explain myself.

"Are you in love with him?" she'd asked me one day as we sat on the porch swing together, slowly rocking back and forth.

I lowered my head, feeling the shame wash over me. "I care for him and respect him very much, but..."

"He loves you, Shannon," she'd said, keeping her eyes on the tree-lined street, watching the neighbors walk by. "I see it in his eyes, and I hear it in his voice. He expects you to feel the same way about him."

"But these medical bills—"

She whipped her head toward me, and her eyes flashed brilliantly. "How dare you? I can take care of myself. You can take care of yourself. We don't need his money!"

"But we do," I said. "The more money we have, the better the medical care for you, and a longer healthier life. I'm going to make sure you stay with me as long as possible."

She looked at me for a long time before speaking. "It's not up to you to decide how long I have on this Earth."

I sighed and chose to end the discussion. "I'm sorry. I know how you feel about it, but I'm going through with this."

She stood from the swing and walked almost mournfully back into the house.

"I love you so much, but I raised you better than this, Shannon."

A soft knock came from the other side of the bathroom door, startling me out of my thoughts. I didn't answer but stared at the closed door through the mirror. The knock came again.

"Shannon?"

I looked to the window, and in a brief moment of insanity, wondered if I could make it out that way. Then I told myself I really was being a coward if I left him now. I stared at my reflection again and decided I'd come too far to turn back now. I pinched my arm as hard as I could stand it, bringing tears to my eyes. The knocking sounded again, only more insistent this time. Gray was coming in one way or another. I pinched myself again.

* * *

Gray didn't like the fact that he was standing outside a locked bathroom, and his wife of two hours wouldn't answer him. He knocked a third time.

"Shannon."

He could hear the faucet running and knew that wouldn't be enough to drown out the knocking, so why the hell wouldn't she answer him?

"Shannon, open the door."

A feeling of dread started to creep up his spine slowly, and if she didn't open the door in the next three seconds, he was breaking it down. The hotel had his credit card on file, so they could bill him for the charges.

He stepped back, ready to ram his body into the door when finally it opened. The first thing he noticed was the tears.

"I'm sorry," she said. "I didn't mean to be so long."

He opened his mouth to ask her why she'd been crying. He nearly asked her if she regretted marrying him; he nearly said there was no need to cry if she was upset about the choice she'd made. They could check out in the morning, head to the courthouse, and get the whole thing annulled. Then, suddenly it hit him what the tears were about, and he felt stupid and insensitive. Christ, her aunt's funeral had only been a few months ago.

He pulled her to him and wrapped his arms around her tightly. "It still hurts when you think about her. It's going to continue to hurt for a while until one day when you do think about her it won't be painful at all."

She pulled away and gave him an odd look as if she didn't expect him to guess at the reason.

"Th—Thank you," she said softly.

He looked around the room, seeking something, anything to help him. A woman in tears made him nervous—especially this woman, who for the last several months had shown him she was tougher than she looked. Coming to Charlie's every day or seeing her around town, he got the impression she was naïve and innocent. But, from the moment she'd walked into the sheriff's office late one rainy night, he'd seen something else in her. The way she'd cared for her aunt told him she was a survivor, not at all afraid of this world. She didn't have family money, connections, or pedigree. She was just Shannon Hollis, and he was lost and in love with her.

"Come, sit down," he said, gesturing to the sitting area of

the suite. "I'll order us some dinner, and we can stay in for the night and watch movies. Unless you want to go out?"

A smile tugged at the corners of her mouth. *Thank God.*

"Room service sounds great."

An hour later, they were cuddled together on the bed, eating chocolate cake and watching an action flick. Though he'd been interested in the movie, Gray's attention was on her, and why he suddenly felt awkward around her. They hadn't made love, yet, but he'd wanted to play it safe and leave that entirely up to her. He figured when she was ready, she'd come to him. But this was their wedding night, and he got the feeling this was going to end like all of their dates for the months they'd been courting, with him hard and frustrated with need for her.

"You didn't seem nervous this afternoon," she said, keeping her eyes on the television.

"I wasn't."

She turned and looked at him, smiling. "What makes you so special? Everyone gets pre-wedding jitters."

He shrugged. "I just wasn't."

She kept her eyes on him and waited patiently for him to elaborate. He smiled. "Fine. I couldn't say this before, but since we're already married, I guess it doesn't matter much."

He was finding it hard to look at her, so he kept his eyes on the plate of dessert he was holding.

"I always wanted you, Shannon. When I'd see you around town, and you would run away from me—"

"I never ran—"

"When I was being a jerk to you at Charlie's."

"Gray."

"And when you came to me that night soaking wet from the rain, needing a ride home, I thought: 'she's always right in front of me, but I can't have her.'"

She put the plate of unfinished chocolate cake on the

table beside the bed and faced him again. "Well, you have me now, and you weren't being a jerk."

He scoffed and mocked himself. "It's *Deputy* Spencer."

She smiled and ducked her head. "Well, maybe a bit of a jerk. Anyway, that title doesn't matter anymore, because, in a few days, you'll be Sheriff Spencer."

He shook his head. "I still can't believe the people voted me in."

"I can. They like you, Gray, and I...Jesus, I almost forgot!"

Gray watched with surprise and fascination as she leaped out of bed and began rummaging inside her overnight bag.

"What is it?" he asked, putting his plate aside and sitting up.

She finally unearthed what she was looking for, looked at him, and slowly walked back to the bed, holding a medium-sized, gift-wrapped box in her hands.

He frowned. "What is that?"

"A gift." She held it out to him. "Apparently, the bride and groom exchange wedding presents, too."

His gaze went between her and the box several times before he reached out and took it from her.

"Don't get too excited. It's nothing expensive," she joked.

He gently tore at the wrapping paper and lifted the lid of the black box inside. Underneath the tissue paper was a framed picture. He took it out, studied the image, and was suddenly so embarrassed by the lump in his throat that he didn't say anything for a long while.

It was a photograph of fifteen men and women, deputies, secretaries, dispatch operators, all in uniform and beaming smiles at the camera. Front and center was a banner they held that read: *Welcome Sheriff Spencer.*

When he felt comfortable enough to speak without making a fool of himself, he looked up at her.

"You did this?"

Apparently, his long silence had made her uncomfortable because she hesitated before slowly nodding.

"You were off one day, and it was just after they announced the results of the election. I borrowed my aunt's camera and arranged a time when everyone could meet to take the picture."

He held the picture with one hand and used his free hand to take hold of her wrist, gently pulling her forward until she was close enough for him to kiss her full, soft lips.

* * *

I looked over at Gray, who was still fully dressed, lying over the covers asleep, and I felt terrible. After I'd given him the picture, he thanked me with a kiss that screamed sexy, which I abruptly ended, and the two of us had gone back to watching the movie.

This was his wedding night, for Christ's sake, and just because I didn't take it seriously didn't mean he didn't. I should have at least made some sort of effort, maybe bought some sexy lingerie to show off for him. Isn't that what brides did for their grooms just before letting them tear it off and make love to them?

Yeah, I felt like a piece of crap. We had spent our short courtship not going any further than kissing, so of course, the man expected me to give up the goodies now that I was his wife. Instead, I was content to let him fall asleep and deal with marital relations later. But the truth was, wedding night or not, I wasn't sure if I'd ever be ready to give myself to Gray. It wasn't about the sex because I'd lost my virginity my first year in college to a guy who'd dumped me the moment I gave him what he wanted. There had been a couple of others after him, so I didn't doubt my experience. I just couldn't trust myself around Gray.

Growing up, I admired him from afar, as we didn't have many opportunities to get to know each other. But when I'd dropped out of college to come home and care for my aunt, I'd been struck by the man he'd become. Tall, with broad shoulders, a strong build, firm jaw, and arresting honey-brown eyes that were just a shade lighter than mine. He wasn't movie-star gorgeous like Cody. Gray's was a subtle handsomeness, enough to get a woman to notice, but not knock her over with it. But more than that, Gray had a prowess about him that was both intriguing and terrifying. He would be an unselfish lover but demanding in other ways. Even now, in his sleep, his heat commanded my attention. I wasn't afraid of him, but of his effect on me.

I'd been staring at him, watching him so intently, that when he opened his eyes, I couldn't even look away.

"Have you looked your fill?" he asked.

Not in a million years, I thought, but said aloud, "I—I think so."

He raised his arms to rest his hands on the back of his head. "Then touch me."

The wicked gleam in his eyes was daring me to make this next move into what was unknown territory between us.

Would he burn me? Probably, but the truth was I wanted so badly to be burned by him. I rose to my knees to climb atop and straddle him. Gray didn't move any part of his body. Even his eyes remained still, trained on my face as I placed my hands on his shoulders and slowly brought them down to the middle of his torso. There, I grabbed the hem of his shirt and pulled it up over his head to expose his bare chest to me. I repeated the motion of my hands, this time letting my fingertips trail over his skin. He immediately grew hard beneath me. I looked at him, excited to see the hunger in his eyes.

"Whenever you're ready," he said.

I pulled my own top over my head and unhooked my bra. I could feel my nipples growing hard from the coolness of the air conditioning hitting my bare skin. Gray's look intensified.

"Touch me first," I commanded and barely got the words out before he sat up and covered my breasts with his hands.

I let him knead and massage his fill, moaning as his rough palms circled my sensitive nipples.

"Taste me," I whispered.

He wrapped his arms tightly around my waist and brought his wet mouth to my breasts. I tossed my head back and moaned louder. His tongue was electric. I cupped the back of his head, ran my hands through his hair and pulled him in closer as my body began to move on its own, circling my hips and rubbing against him until I became impatient for not being able to feel all of him.

He got impatient too because he released his mouth and pushed me down onto the bed. He followed right after me and paused to hover over my body.

"Are you all right?" he asked, his breath coming in quick pants.

"Yes."

"Good, because I've wanted this for too long, and I'm not stopping."

I felt his urgency as he tugged off my panties and entered me in one swift move. We moaned together at the first feel of each other, and he wasted no time in setting the rhythm and pace. I was overwhelmed by him, unable to get enough, and it surprised and frightened me, while he watched me with an intensity that held me captive. He wanted me to feel as good as he did, but there was something else there. He hadn't come into this marriage on false pretenses. He loved me, and that thought alone brought tears to my eyes because I knew I didn't deserve it. Yet, I still clung to him, wanting this moment to last, wanting that look in his eyes to last because if he ever found out the truth, I'd never see it again.

He moved inside of me with relentless strokes, and I kept my legs tight about his waist, prolonging the moment and the feel of him. It wasn't long before a shattering climax ripped through me, and I cried out his name in surrender. Gray kept the pace going until he was moaning and coming right behind me. When he fell beside me and laid his head against my breasts, I knew I was in trouble. I did not marry this man for love, but my intentions were changing with each passing moment.

Gray turned off the lamp switch and then reached for me in the dark to hold me close. For a long time, we stayed that way, listening to the sounds of our breathing in cadence, slowing to a steady pace. We would both be asleep soon.

Then Gray spoke out in the dark. "Oh, yeah," he said, as though he just remembered. "I have a wedding present for you, too."

CHAPTER THIRTEEN

"I still don't understand why you dragged me out here, Gray. I've already seen the crime scene photos."

Gretchen wrapped her arms around her light wool coat to protect against the brisk autumn morning. When Gray got a call from his crime scene tech, he called Gretchen down to hear the newest evidence. After all, she would be prosecuting the murderer if and when he or she would be caught. He ignored her annoyance and stood beside Deputy Leah Collins and his crime scene investigator.

"Tell me what you see."

The young man used a pointer to demonstrate where the body of Frank Miles lay two days before.

"When we found the body, there were drops of blood on the leaves where his body lay."

Gray nodded. He knew it had been an exasperating routine for his investigators to pick up every last dried leaf as evidence. But it was fall now in Gypsy Bay, and they couldn't risk the leaves blowing away that might have any type of

DNA evidence on them, whether it be the victim's or the murderer's.

"But I noticed there wasn't enough blood to justify the three fatal wounds to the chest."

Gray could sense Gretchen's interest pick up at those words and felt her moving in closer behind them to listen.

"Also, the way the body was positioned, it doesn't fit the justification of a man who'd been shot three times." The investigator paused to pull out a photo of the victim lying at the crime scene. "See how the body is lying? It's too perfect. Three shots to the chest would have this man staggering back and falling down not as neatly as you see here in the photograph."

"What are you saying?" Gretchen asked.

Deputy Collins turned to her. "The victim was killed somewhere else, and his body was placed here. This crime scene was staged."

Gray looked at the ADA, who looked to him and then turned to walk away.

"Thanks, Terry," Gray said to his crime scene tech and started to go after Gretchen before he was stopped by his deputy's hand on his arm.

"What was that about, Gray?" Leah asked. "You knew this scene was staged the moment we discovered it, didn't you?"

"Yes."

"Why the show?"

"To prove a point."

She nodded toward Gretchen, who was now standing at the edge of the hill overlooking the forest and lake. "She's going after your ex-wife, isn't she?"

Gray gave a non-committal nod. "She is leaning toward Shannon as a suspect, yes."

"But you don't think, or don't want to believe she did this."

Gray didn't answer.

"With all due respect, Sheriff, I don't like being used—"

"That's not what I meant—"

"But I agree we should be looking at other suspects," she continued. "So I'll let this one go."

He nodded his understanding and started to apologize when his phone sounded. He removed it from his holster, looked at the display, and recognized the number to Charlie's restaurant.

"Sheriff Spencer."

"Hi, Gray, it's Shannon."

He couldn't stop the rush of excitement that went straight to his loins at the sound of her voice. Before he embarrassed himself in front of his deputy, he raised one finger to her and turned to walk away.

"Hey. What's going on?"

"I'm on break right now and wanted to call and tell you I did what you asked. I went through everything I could in the house."

"Thank you for doing that. I know it might be painful going through your aunt's things."

"Not so much. I had good memories here, so it was nice to relive them. It was the other things, that…well, you know."

He looked up at the sky for a moment and then back down. "Yeah, I know."

He'd resisted looking at their wedding photos from that little place in San Francisco when he had movers box her things up. He didn't want to see her in that simple dress she'd picked up just for that occasion.

Silence fell between them, and Gray could sense there was more she needed to say but didn't know how to say it.

"What is it?"

"Um, the one thing I couldn't account for was my engagement ring."

"Yeah, that's because I have it."

Silence followed again, and suddenly he felt like he'd said the wrong thing.

"You left it in our—my house, remember? I put it with my mother's things." He lowered his voice even more. "Look, Shannon, it's been in the family for six generations—"

"It's fine," she said. "I remember now."

"Gray!"

He turned to see Gretchen waving to him, indicating she was ready to head back into town. He raised one finger to indicate she hold on for a moment longer.

"There's one other thing," Shannon said.

He wanted to explain more about her engagement ring. He wanted her to understand that he didn't want it back, but it seemed that neither did she.

"If this case you're working is going in the direction I think it's going, you're going to find two more pieces of jewelry that Cody gave to me, earrings and a necklace. I don't have them."

She left the rest unsaid. *He* was supposed to have them, but the last thing he remembered about that jewelry set was packing it away with the intention to donate it to a second-hand store. He had been so overtaken by jealousy at the thought of her wearing a gift from another man, he never even wanted to see them again. But with everything that had happened, he never donated them. Could he have mistakenly packed them up with Shannon's things and sent them to her Aunt's house?

"I have to go," he said. "Let me know if anything else comes up."

"I will. Be careful."

She always used to tell him that when they were married, and he was working late. He didn't like the flood of memories that haunted him every time he saw or spoke to her, yet at the same time, he welcomed and relished them.

"You too."

He hung up and turned back to Deputy Collins. "I'm going to give Gretchen a ride back to town."

"Go," she said. "I'll be all right here, but be careful with her."

"With Gretchen?"

Leah nodded. "From the brief time I've known her, I can sense she likes to win, and people who like to win sometimes can't help themselves from doing anything to see that they keep on winning."

He gave a small salute and then headed down the hill to his SUV where Gretchen was now waiting. He unlocked the car, and they both climbed inside. As soon as the doors shut, she turned to him.

"I don't care what was said up there. Shannon Spencer doesn't have an alibi for that night, and if you don't bring her in for questioning, I'll make sure someone else does."

Gray sighed. "You've threatened to remove me from this case before. It doesn't carry quite the same punch as the first time."

"So, you don't care?"

He turned the key in the ignition and then sat back, leaned against the headrest, and closed his eyes briefly at the sound of hurt in Shannon's voice when he'd told her he'd kept her engagement ring.

Then groaning aloud, he put the car in gear. "I get the feeling, as this case progresses, I'm going to beg you to stop threatening and just do it."

"You could remove yourself," she said, as they drove off.

Gray kept his eyes straight ahead, focused on the road, but his mind was still on the crime scene. If it was staged, where exactly had Frank Miles been killed and what did Shannon's missing jewelry have to do with it?

He shook his head. "I don't know how to do that."

CHAPTER FOURTEEN

I resisted the urge to turn and give Gray and his beautiful companion any attention as I filled a customer's order for steak and eggs. It was too late, of course. I'd spotted the two as soon as they walked into the restaurant. Hell, everyone in the place had noticed, and if I wasn't crazy, I swore I heard a hushed breath sweep over the crowd at the fact that Gypsy Bay's equivalent of the power couple had graced Charlie's with their presence.

I took a deep breath and recognized my cattiness for what it was. I was still upset about the last conversation I'd had with Gray. The man had a right to take back his engagement ring, especially an heirloom that had been in his family for generations. Still, it was painful to hear that the one material object I'd cherished the most during my marriage was gone.

It's not like you gave him a choice, I reminded myself. Gray had come up to that awful place every weekend for an entire year, begging me to tell him why I'd shot his brother, and every single time, he left without an answer. But he didn't understand. I couldn't look at him anymore after that night without seeing the pain and betrayal. Someone he loved had died, and the reasons why would only bring him more pain.

Then one day, he stopped coming to see me, and I'd pretended to be relieved. That is until his lawyer showed up with divorce papers, and as much as I'd been expecting it, that moment had destroyed me.

"Mr. Spencer wanted to come and deliver these to you himself," the older man had said to me, who had no doubt been the Spencer family lawyer for decades.

I just sat there, staring at the papers he placed in front of me, and all I could focus on was the bold black writing at the top of the page: *Dissolution of Marriage.*

The lawyer cleared his throat. "Mrs. Spencer, there was never a prenuptial agreement signed between you and Mr. Spencer, but due to the nature of your conviction, I'm obligated to tell you that you have no claim to—"

"I don't want anything," I'd said abruptly and grabbed for the pen resting on the table. I signed my name in a rush, stood, and called out for the guard to come and get me. Once back inside my cell, I'd looked around at the tiny four walls and then suddenly felt my body begin to weaken. I dropped to the foot of the bed, bunched my knees up to my chest and gave into the sobs that racked through me.

Later, I was surprised at the fact that the cell block had been eerily quiet that entire time. Some women, who had been in prison for years and had the hope knocked out of them would have yelled for me to "shut the fuck up," but no one called out or said anything, and out of respect for the female gender, allowed me to get my pain out in the most natural way.

"Wake up, sleeping beauty. I need that computer."

I gladly came away from that day and stood to the side to let Marissa put her own orders in.

"Everything okay?" Marissa asked, focused on the touch

screen monitor where she furiously put in drink and food orders.

I didn't respond but risked a glance over at Gray's table. The two were engrossed in their meal and whatever it was they were discussing. I turned back only to find Marissa staring right back at me.

"What?"

She shook her head and printed out a receipt for one of her customers. "Her name is Gretchen Miller, and she's an Assistant County Prosecutor."

"I know who she is," I said indignantly. "Did I ask who she is?"

Before my arrest, I'd only come into contact with Gretchen Miller very briefly at a little coffee shop in town. We both seemed to share a liking for caramel macchiato, but as far as I could remember, our acquaintance never went any further than the occasional hello when we'd see each other in the mornings. She was the successful, black woman I had aspired to be, but could never make happen in my own life. With her accomplishments, confidence and independence, I had always thought she was the type of woman Gray would find irresistible, but with the way he adored me, I never allowed the green-eyed monster inside of me to rise. Until now. Had they begun seeing each other when I left?

Marissa put the receipt into a leather billfold and leaned forward to kiss me on the cheek. "Number one: It's time for your break; I'll cover you. Number two: Yes, I do think he's a complete asshole for bringing her here. You know what you need? Some time away. Why don't you borrow the cabin for a weekend?"

I smiled, thinking of memories with Marissa, Jeremy, and old friends from high school when we'd spend summer days at her parents' cabin eating barbecue and swimming in the lake.

"The back patio door lock needs fixing, but other than that, it's all ready for you to make yourself right at home and get away from here and all the fucking gossiping."

She pulled out a specially made key for the cabin, red with white polka dots, and dangled it in front of me.

"Take it," she urged. "You deserve some me time for yourself."

As much as I was tempted by the offer, I shook my head. I couldn't tell her that leaving would interfere with why I returned to Gypsy Bay in the first place.

"Thanks, but I've had enough me time in prison."

"You'll change your mind."

She winked and walked away. I smiled and headed to the back of the restaurant to grab my jacket out of my locker, just like I did every night during my break. I went outside by way of the kitchen and was met with a cool breeze floating in off the lake. Most of the girls came out this way to sit on the benches and have a cigarette, but I kept walking down the path that led to the trees and the lake beyond. I stopped just before reaching the trees and stood waiting. I reached into my jacket pocket and clutched the gun I kept tucked in there.

"Come on, you bastard," I whispered against the breeze. "I know you see me."

"What was that?"

I whirled around and saw Gretchen Miller standing a few feet away, holding her curly strands out of her face. I eyed the statuesque woman from head to toe, and to my horror, realized this really was the woman Gray was supposed to marry. I'd read about Gretchen Miller and knew her family came from money, too. Brains and pedigree —the Spencers would have been proud. It certainly would have been better for Gray. Cody would probably still be alive, and he wouldn't have been saddled with a convict for an ex-wife.

"I was talking to myself. It's a habit I've had for a long time now."

"Something you picked up in Chowchilla?"

I ignored that and turned my gaze back to the trees. I heard the leaves rustling behind me and knew the woman was taking a few steps toward me.

"How are you getting along being back in Gypsy Bay?"

I stared at her. I didn't say anything, but the look I gave was clear, and Gretchen picked up on it right away.

"I only ask because your name is infamous around here. It can be hard coming back." She dropped her head, and whisks of dark curls fell to her face, and I wondered if she always tried to be sexy or if it just came naturally.

"Why did you come back?"

I wrapped my jacket around my body tighter, careful not to let the shape of the gun show, and took a couple of steps toward her. When I was close enough to her face, I spoke in a low tone.

"I'm going to ask you the same thing: Why are you here? Did Gray send you? Did he think that maybe if it was just us girls, I'd be more apt to confess something?"

"No, I didn't."

We both turned to see Gray standing a few feet away. I ignored the slight tug in my belly at the way he seemed to always look so good in his jeans. I knew for a fact being sexy was just part of Gray's nature. He couldn't help it.

He kept his hard eyes on me but called to Gretchen. "You ready?"

"Sure." Gretchen dug in her purse and came up with a business card, which she handed to me. "We should talk sometime. You and I can meet at that coffeehouse we like. We have a lot more in common than you think."

With that parting remark, I watched as the two headed back toward the parking lot to get in Gray's truck and drive away. I put the card in my back pocket and started to head back inside. That's when I heard it.

I turned and looked toward the trees but could see only darkness, and the wind kicked up again, masking whatever noises would follow. But just before the silence had been broken, I knew I'd heard that same rustle of footsteps among the leaves.

* * *

"I can't believe she was bold enough to confront you like that," Marissa said for the hundredth time since I walked back into the diner and told her about the encounter with Gretchen Miller. Even now, as we were in Marissa's car headed to my home, she still couldn't stop talking about it.

"What did she say to you?"

"She didn't say much. I get the feeling she wanted to intimidate me more than anything."

Marissa snorted. "What? Did she believe you were going to confess to the murder of that hiker?"

I laid my head back against the headrest and closed my eyes. "I guess. Maybe I'll always be the first suspect when a murder happens anywhere near Gypsy Bay."

I could feel Marissa staring at me but refused to acknowledge her.

"Good thing Gray came out when he did."

I gave a soft chuckle and this time looked at her. "This from the woman who called him an asshole not even two hours ago."

"Yes, he is an asshole for bringing Miss America to the diner, knowing his ex-wife would be there."

"He's free to have dinner with whoever he wants. The key word is *ex-wife*."

"But, he's not the type to have a woman do his bidding for

him," Marissa continued. "If Gray wanted to ask you questions, he would do it himself. He is the sheriff, after all."

The car went silent after that, and I knew there was something more on Marissa's mind.

"What's wrong?"

She turned to me and then back to the road ahead. "You're never going to tell anyone, are you?"

"Tell what?"

"Don't do that, Shannon. You know exactly what I'm talking about. You went away for three years, and I know why, but I don't really know *why*."

I rolled the window down until the air was blowing directly on my face. It was chilly outside, but I was suddenly feeling warm—and trapped.

"I was there that day when you spilled glasses of lemonade all over your future husband, remember? You were so mortified after that and scared that man would hate you forever."

"Seriously, Marissa? Are you really going that far back?"

"I also remember nights when you wouldn't let me take you home. A blue Ferrari would pull up outside the diner, and everybody knew who it belonged to."

I turned to her, my eyes flashing. "Nothing was going on between Cody and me. At least not what you're thinking."

"I know that. But there was something because every time he did pull up, you looked so afraid."

I kept my eyes on Marissa, who kept her eyes on the road as she continued on. "I look back now and think to myself what kind of friend was I to let you get in that car with him? I should've stopped you or something. But when you and Gray were married, I thought everything would be fine. He adored you, and you were completely smitten with him. Then, not even a year later, you're being charged for Cody's murder, and I knew it had never ended."

My house came into view. Marissa pulled into the driveway and shut off the engine. Still, she kept her eyes straight ahead.

I leaned forward and put my arms around Marissa's neck, kissed her on the cheek, and laid my head on her shoulder. "You know it wasn't your fault. You know that."

Marissa put a hand over my arm. "I just wish you'd tell me why you did it." Then she added, barely on a whisper, "If you did it."

I had closed my eyes as I was resting on her shoulder, but with those words, I slowly opened them, lifted my head, and stared at my friend.

"What did you say?"

Marissa stared right back and then began to smile. "Turn on the light once you get inside. I'll see you tomorrow."

We sat there for just a moment longer, wondering what secrets the other knew, and then I started to pull away, but my hair got caught in the gold chain around Marissa's neck. Marissa instantly grabbed for the chain and gently untangled my hair.

"This thing is always getting in the way," she said.

I smiled, thanked her for the ride, and climbed out of the car. I walked up the steps to my front porch, unlocked the door, and turned to wave goodbye. That was the moment I was pulled roughly inside the house.

he breath was knocked out of me the moment I was pulled inside. I was thrown to the side of the room and into the coffee table, which rested in the middle of the living room. I hit my side against the wooden corner and cried out. As I tried to get my bearings, I watched in horror as my attacker kicked the door shut behind him, effectively cutting out the only light from the street lamps outside and plunging us both into darkness. The next sound I heard was the click of the lock, and I knew I had to get out of there fast.

I held my side and tried to sit up, but he moved fast. He got a grip of my hair and pulled so tight I thought he would rip it out by the root. Then he slapped me hard. The assault shocked and frightened me at the same time, but before I could recover, he slapped me again, and this time I tasted blood. He slapped me once more, and I could feel my vision begin to blur.

Don't pass out. Don't pass out.

There came a loud knock against the front door.

"Shannon, open the door! Are you all right? Open the fucking door!"

Marissa. Thank God she hadn't driven away. I screamed, hoping it would spring her into action. I then heard her footsteps as she ran back down the porch steps, more than likely going to get her cell phone from her car.

But my momentary feeling of victory was overshadowed when I was rewarded in the next instant with a punch to the side of my head. He released my hair, and I fell to the floor. He started kicking me with the toe of his boot. On instinct, I protected my stomach and curled inward, but he kept kicking and kicking, and I knew if I stayed this way, I would pass out from the pain alone.

I turned to my side and began moving along the floor, feeling for something, anything I could use as a weapon. That left my side exposed to his boot. With each kick, I heard his grunt of satisfaction.

The gun.

Before we left Charlie's that night, I had put the gun in my purse. *Goddammit, where is my purse?* When I was flung inside, my purse had landed somewhere in the room, but it was so dark, I had no idea where it could be. I could only reach for what was nearby that would have fallen to the floor when I landed against the coffee table, and I threw at this bastard whatever my hands touched: magazines, the remote control, my aunt's wooden bowls. My hand gripped the base of a small lamp, and I threw it with all my strength. But my eyes had not fully adjusted to the darkness, and I was in such pain my aim was off. The lamp crashed against the wall somewhere behind him.

Find something. He's going to kill you. Find something!

I reached and reached but felt nothing but the carpet fibers under my hands, and he just kept kicking. I was in tears now, crying and screaming.

Find something, please!

I found something. As soon as I felt it, I gripped it like a lifeline. That's when my attacker bent over and took me by the waist to lift me up. His arms were wrapped tightly around me, skyrocketing the pain to my injured bones. He lifted me, and I kicked my legs wildly, trying to strike wherever I could. He tightened his hold around me, turned, and pushed me against the fireplace. My back slammed into the mantel, and I dropped like a rag doll. The moment I hit the floor, I knew I was losing consciousness. He knelt down and leaned over me, and I could now see he was wearing a mask. I would wonder later what he must have been thinking as he just seemed to stare at me, studying me.

The sound of sirens in the distance seemed to distract him, and he looked up. I took that instant to flip the lid on the mace I'd kept in my clutches when he lifted me off the floor. I brought my hand up. The movement caused him to look back down at me, which is exactly what I wanted. I turned my head to the side, closed my eyes, and sprayed for all I was worth.

Even more beautiful than the sound of the sirens were his screams as the mace blinded his eyes. I began coughing from the spray and used the last of my strength to crawl away to the corner of the room. I wanted desperately to hit him with something, but the assault had completely immobilized me. Sitting in the corner of the room, I watched as he clutched at his eyes and began flinging objects from the mantel. I tried to detect his voice over the screams, but it was unrecognizable.

The sirens grew louder, and his screams and curses had turned into groans. He felt his way along the walls, heading for the rear of the house. I watched him go and listened for the sound of the patio door off the kitchen to open and slam shut.

Moments later, my front door crashed open, and sheriff's deputies flooded my home.

* * *

Gray watched her as she sat on the hospital bed, lifted her shirt, and gingerly moved her hand along the bandage wrapped around her stomach.

"Jesus," she hissed through clenched teeth and then looked up to find him standing in the doorway to her room.

"It's not as bad as it looks," she said in a rush.

He didn't reply but strode to her bed to stand directly in front of her. He looked at her for a moment and then down to the bandage. He ran his fingers along the opposite side of her stomach. She inhaled a breath as if waiting for the imminent pain to shoot through her, but she didn't cry out.

"Does this side hurt, too?" he asked gently.

"No. My left side got the brunt of his kicks."

He looked at her again, not bothering to mask the cold fury he felt coursing through his body. He was going to find this guy. He was going to find him and hurt him.

"Please, don't blame yourself, Gray," she said, lowering her shirt. "You can't be everywhere."

"No, but I should have followed my first instinct to keep watch over you. I won't make that mistake again."

She glared at him. "What are you doing here, anyway? I thought you were off duty."

"I was. One of the guys called me as soon as they heard it was you who was attacked."

"So I ruined your night with Ms. Miller of the County Prosecutor's office. Sorry about that."

"You didn't." He studied her for a moment and then felt the need to continue. "There's nothing going on between her and me."

He wanted to tell her that his brief fling with Gretchen had been months after their divorce was finalized, but she had turned away from him.

"You didn't have to come down here. I gave one of the deputies my statement already," she said. "I wasn't able to ID the guy. It was dark, and he wore a mask, so I doubt they'll have much to go on in finding him."

"It won't stop me from looking."

She snorted a laugh. "I know. You're still relentless with every case you take on."

He wasn't in the mood to go down memory lane with her. He did enough of that on his own, late at night when he was alone in that big house. Besides, he had too much on his mind, namely the fact that he hadn't been there when she needed him. She was putting on a good front, but he knew without a doubt she must have been frightened for her life.

"Why didn't you tell me this happened before?"

A look of surprise crossed her face, but it changed quickly to resignation. "I should have guessed. Marissa never could hold water."

"She didn't tell me. It slipped out when she was waiting on one of my men at Charlie's."

Shannon kept quiet, keeping her eyes lowered.

"I shouldn't have had to hear it secondhand."

She looked as though she was trying to escape him but couldn't get off the bed without hurting herself. She groaned aloud. "Gray, please stop."

That pissed him off, and he erupted with the anger he'd barely been able to control. "Stop what? What the hell is the matter with you? Someone broke into your house twice. This time you were assaulted, nearly killed, and you're pissed at me for wanting to know about it?"

She shook her head and looked away from him. Something was wrong here. It was one thing to be independent, but she was acting as if she wanted to be attacked. She seemed to be constantly tempting fate, just like this evening when he'd found her outside with Gretchen standing at the edge of the forest. Before Gretchen had come out, she'd been standing out there alone, in the near dark, looking as if she were daring someone to do something to her.

He hooked a finger underneath her chin and turned her to face him the way he used to when he wanted her full attention.

"What are you doing, Shannon?"

A throat cleared, and they both turned to see Marissa eyeing them cautiously, as though she were deciding whether to stand back or intrude.

"Hi," Shannon said, smiling at her friend.

Gray released her chin and stepped back as Marissa moved slowly into the room and toward them. She looked from Shannon to him.

"Hi, Sheriff."

He nodded a greeting. "I'm glad you were there."

"Yeah, me too." Then she eyed Shannon. "I hear you've got severe bruising, but nothing was broken."

Shannon nodded, darting a look at Gray. "Yeah, I was pretty lucky."

"Good, because I'm springing you free. The doctor will be here any minute to have you sign paperwork and give you some scripts for the good stuff."

Silence fell, and Marissa divided a look between the two of them again before settling on him.

"I'll take care of her, Gray. Don't worry."

He felt like he was being dismissed, but he didn't want to go. He didn't want to let her out of his sight for fear that the next time someone came for her, they'd finish the job. But it was a snowball's chance in hell he'd get the option of carrying her out of the hospital and back to his home where he would watch over her and make sure no one ever hurt her again.

So, as much as it pained him to let her out of his sight, he would for now. Besides, he'd gotten what he needed from her when he looked into her eyes. She was determined to bait a killer, and the only reason she would do that is if she was damn sure a killer was coming for her.

CHAPTER SIXTEEN

Five years ago…

"So, you're still alive."

Gray turned from his computer monitor and grinned at his brother, standing in the doorway to his office.

"I thought maybe I might have to pay you a visit to make sure your wife hadn't killed you," Cody said, stepping forward and embracing Gray with a back-slapping hug when he stood.

"How have you been?" Gray asked.

"How have *I* been? Shit, you're the one who suddenly just up and elopes to San Francisco without so much as a phone call to your baby brother. Add to that, you've been basically MIA for two weeks. I called your office on a whim, and your assistant surprised the hell out of me when she told me you were on duty today."

Gray knew he was wearing a stupid grin on his face, but he couldn't do anything but shrug. Apparently, his good mood was contagious, because soon after, Cody was wearing a grin of his own.

"Jesus. And everybody thought you had ice water in your veins. Now, look at you."

He sat down in one of the chairs in front of Gray's desk and leaned back with a studious expression.

"Is she good for you?"

"Yeah," Gray said, returning to his own seat. "She is."

"So, where is she? I doubt she's still working at Charlie's."

"At home. Probably meeting with the architect right now to go over the floor plans for the house."

Cody's grin dropped a fraction. "You bought her a house?"

"If you want to call it that. We practically have to gut it out." He paused, noticed Cody's curious frown, and felt the need to explain. "I've been looking to buy a house for a long time now. I thought maybe we'd sell Mom and Dad's place, and you and I split the profit."

Cody nodded, lacing his fingers together and resting them on his stomach. "Sure, we can do that."

Then he went silent again, and his face became unreadable.

"What is it, Cody?"

Cody shook his head as if emerging from a trance. "It's just good to see you finally happy. Charlie's doesn't carry champagne, but I can buy you a beer to celebrate."

Gray shook his head. "I'm on duty. Besides, I should be toasting you. It's been nearly a month, and I haven't had to smooth Mike's feathers because you harassed him for more money. What's going on? Did you get a job?"

Cody nodded and studied the surface of the wooden desk between them. "In a manner of speaking."

"What's that supposed to mean?"

Cody smiled. "Forget it. Let's just say I'm keeping myself busy these days."

Gray shrugged. "Whatever. I'm just glad to hear it."

Silence rested, and Gray knew there was more on Cody's mind and decided to wait him out.

"I always thought you'd come and tell me when you found the woman of your dreams. Hell, I thought I'd be best man at your wedding one day. But considering the way I've been acting, I can understand why you eloped without telling me."

Gray sighed. "That's got nothing to do with it. An elopement is supposed to be secret."

Cody raised a hand to forestall any more objections. "Still, if I hadn't been such a self-absorbed asshole this past year, I would have seen that something has changed in you. So, in addition to congratulations, I came to tell you I'm sorry."

Gray nodded, rose from his desk again, and embraced his brother. "We didn't hug this much even when Mom and Dad died."

Cody returned the embrace and then stepped back. "I'll pay a visit to the Missus as soon as I can. I want to congratulate her myself and give her a wedding present."

"If Shannon's not home, you can almost always find her at the construction site. I think maybe she missed her calling as a contractor."

Cody turned for the door, stopped, and turned back around. "Look, Gray, this is none of my business, and you can tell me to fuck off if you want."

"What is it?"

"Did you get a pre-nup?"

Gray rapped a knuckle against his desk and chuckled to himself. "You're the first

person with big enough balls to ask me that."

"I'm also family."

"She offered, and I declined. Call me a fool, but I honestly don't think she cares about that."

Cody lowered his head and muttered something under his breath.

"What was that?"

Gray watched as his younger brother raised his head with that charming smile back in place. "I think you might be right."

He walked out, and Gray frowned at the closed door.

That's not what you said.

CHAPTER SEVENTEEN

*J*ason thrashed through the trees, caught himself in a tangle of brush, and cursed as he flung himself free and nearly toppled to the ground. When he finally righted himself, he looked around and realized he was somewhere in the dense forest and had lost sight of the campsite.

"Great," he muttered to himself. As soon as he got back to San Francisco, he was kicking Sam's ass. This was all his fault anyway.

Okay, well maybe it was partly Jason's fault. He was the one who asked Sam to set him up with one of Diane's hot friends. He'd needed to show his ex he could move on just as fast as she could, and he thought he'd get the chance when Sam came to him with the idea of a double date camping trip. Jason liked the idea, but made Sam promise him the girl was super-hot; otherwise, there would be no escape, and his weekend would fucking suck.

"Trust me," was all Sam had said, and Jason did after getting one look at Diane. She was almost as good-looking as his ex, and he couldn't wait to meet her friend, especially after Sam told him she was a doctor. Even better.

But when he was introduced to Tracy, he gave Sam a look that said, *When this is over, you and I are going to have a talk about the meaning of super-hot. Right after I kick your ass.*

She was this nerdy, bookish type, and at first, he'd thought, with some hope, she'd be one of those hot librarian types that once they took off their glasses and let their hair swing loose, they'd turn into every man's fantasy. But she wasn't much to look at with or without her glasses. Her hair wasn't long and flowing like his ex's. In fact, it was cut too short in his opinion. The only thing he had left to hope for was that she had a killer body, but there was no chance of him getting a peek because, from the moment they all piled into Sam's car, she treated him like a pariah.

Damn, wasn't it just his luck that a woman he wasn't even remotely interested in was treating him like an annoying pest? A few times already, he'd caught Tracy whispering and giggling to Diane, and he knew they were talking about him.

The long day had turned into night, and then they were all sitting by the fire, drinking and talking about anything. By about the fifth time the two girls whispered to each other, Jason leaned over toward Sam and had his own private conversation.

"What the fuck is her problem?"

Sam looked sheepish, as if this was something he didn't want to get involved in.

Jason could feel himself growing agitated. "What is it?"

Sam cursed under his breath. "She says you're shallow."

"Shallow?"

Sam shrugged. "I don't get it either. Maybe she expected something different, but fuck her. Enjoy the rest of the night and—"

"Hey, Tracy, you're not that hot to be such a bitch. There's shallow for you."

Jason hadn't even realized he'd turned to the giggling girls and spoke out loud. But when he realized everyone was staring at him, all he could do was gulp down the rest of his beer. Then Tracy, obviously having had her feelings hurt, jumped up and stormed off to her tent, followed quickly by Diane, who gave him a hateful look. Then Sam turned to him and started to say something, but Jason had had enough of everybody being so damned sensitive. He was the one with the ruined weekend.

"Don't start with me, man."

Grabbing a new can of beer from the cooler and a flashlight, he stood and walked off in the direction of the woods. Twenty minutes and what had to be a quarter of a mile later, he found a fallen log, sat down, took a drink, and let out a loud burp.

"That's for you, Tracy," he muttered. "Shallow, my ass."

If she wanted to see shallow, she should take a visit to his ex's house—a woman who dumps a good guy as soon as a better-looking and more successful one comes along.

Jason started laughing. He just described the entire female population, didn't he? Stupid bitches.

The crack of a twig caught his attention, but he'd drunk a little too much beer because his reflexes were off. He couldn't tell from which direction the sound came, but he knew it was nearby. He slowly stumbled to his feet and looked around. The sound came again. Definitely someone walking, and they were getting closer.

"Hey, who's there? Let me see you."

He shined his flashlight in every direction but only illuminated the surrounding trees.

"Sam, I can hear your footsteps, you dumbass. You're not surprising me."

He was actually glad his friend had found him out here because he'd lost all sense of direction a long time ago.

"Hey, man, come on out here. I've got an idea. Let's ditch the girls and head back to San Francisco. Aren't you bored with Diane yet?"

Truthfully, he was jealous of his friend. Diane was hot, sexy, and carefree. Just the kind of girl his ex was. The kind of girl he wanted on his arm.

Damn, maybe he was shallow.

There was no movement anymore, and Jason shined his light all around again, expecting to see Sam, or at the very least one of the girls. But that's not whom he saw. The figure was still, standing only a few feet away, clad in black. But the most noticeable thing was the glint of the gun aimed at the middle of his chest.

CHAPTER EIGHTEEN

I sighed. This was pointless and stupid. Gray was a trained law enforcement officer, and I'd made it abundantly clear to him that I didn't need protecting, and here I was, sitting outside his home at nine o'clock in the evening waiting for what? If there was anyone who didn't need protecting, it was Gray Spencer. He'd proven many times during the course of our short marriage that he was capable of taking care of himself and me. I recalled many nights of not being able to sleep soundly until I'd heard his heavy steps walk into the bedroom. Moments later, he climbed into bed beside me and pulled me toward him. It was as though he instinctively knew I needed to feel him, to know he was safe and nearby before I could fully rest. Of course, after he pulled me against him, he wouldn't allow me to sleep just yet. Next, would come his roaming hands to my breasts, my waist, my thighs, and in between my legs. When he began to rub his fingers slowly and gently inside my pussy until I grew wet, I'd move my ass against his groin in invitation, and we were off.

I cursed to myself. The memory was making me restless,

and that wasn't at all why I'd come here. Maybe I should just go knock on his door and tell him everything. Then he could look out for himself. That is, if he believed me.

This was the second time I'd spent a few hours of my day off following him around, suspecting that he was being targeted by...by a ghost. Yes, ask anyone in Gypsy Bay, and they would swear that Cody Spencer was dead, and I'd killed him. But a body was never found, and until one surfaced, I had to go on believing my enemy was still alive and not finished with Gray or me.

The first afternoon I'd trailed Gray, I followed him to the cliffs where the accident happened that night. I hadn't followed him all the way up the mountain, knowing he would see my car, but I knew where he was going. I held out hope that maybe he also believed his brother was still alive and would be willing to listen to what I had to say. But nearly an hour went by, and Gray hadn't come back down the road. Taking a risk, I drove up to the cliffs, parked several hundred feet from his truck, and walked the rest of the way.

When I got to his truck, he wasn't inside. I looked around, waiting for him to catch me spying on him. Then I looked toward the railing that had since been fixed and stepped toward it. Peering over the railing, I nearly gasped when I spotted Gray sitting on one of the rocky cliff holds, staring down at the crashing waves below.

At first, I'd thought he was mourning, remembering the good times with Cody and, then I noticed a pen and a notepad in his hands. He was trying to remember, and I couldn't let that happen. I went back to my car, my heart filling with dread, but not sure what I could do to make Gray bury the truth.

A white Mercedes cruised down the road, jarring me from my thoughts as it turned into the large circular drive-way. Then a beautiful, familiar-looking woman with dark curly tresses stepped out of the car in an expensive-looking tan linen suit. She chirped the alarm and walked up to the front door as if she belonged there. She rang the doorbell, and in a few moments, Gray's tall and broad silhouette framed the open doorway. They exchanged a lingering kiss and a few words until, finally, he invited her inside.

"Brilliant stakeout, Shannon," I muttered to myself. Not only was I spying on Gray, but I was now spying on Gray and a woman who no doubt was his lover, if not now, definitely in the past. I was officially taking home the crown of scorned and clichéd ex-wife.

Turning on the ignition, I supposed I should thank the amazing Gretchen for showing up. No harm would come to Gray tonight if she was there with him all night. I drove away, looking through the rearview mirror at what used to be my home, and wondered just how much longer I was going to go on torturing myself.

* * *

As soon as Gray closed the door behind Gretchen, she attacked him again with another searing kiss. He took her by the shoulders and pulled her away, trying to breathe in air.

"What's got into you?"

"You know I have this fetish for being watched," she said, smiling. "I couldn't help it with the Peeping Tom outside."

"What Peeping Tom?"

She shrugged. "There's a car a few feet from here. It looked out of place in a neighborhood like this, so I figured you've got a spy on your hands."

He frowned, reaching past her, and yanked open the door. He scanned the darkness only to see fading tail lights round a corner and go out of sight. He closed the door again and locked it.

"Could you see who it was?" he asked.

She shook her head. "Too dark. If you're worried about your safety, tough guy, change these old locks. You've had them for years, and they're too easy to pick. Believe me, I've tried."

"I've got plenty of guns in this house. Besides, I'm relying on the fact that no one is stupid enough to break into the sheriff's house."

"So, if it's not your safety you're concerned about, it's us." Then she laughed and strode past him into his office and to the wet bar. "Don't worry, Sheriff Spencer. Everyone in this town already knows about our brief fling. It's ancient history."

She made herself a vodka tonic with lots of ice and sipped it. She then eyed him as he slowly came into the office, his hands in the pockets of his jeans with a frown still on his face.

She put the drink down on the desk and rounded it, before settling herself into one of the visitors' chairs. "Oh, I get it."

He looked at her sharply. "Get what?"

She crossed her legs in a lazy fashion that screamed sexy. "Everybody knows, but her."

He remained silent, not wanting to confirm she was right.

She sighed. "Gray, you were divorced, and she was in prison. You have nothing to feel guilty about."

"Did you come here for a reason?"

She picked up her glass and held it up, examining it. "You'd think I'd have plans on a Friday night, but I don't, so I thought I'd look in on an old friend and colleague."

"You didn't need to. I'm all right."

She studied his rigid stance and smiled genuinely. "Relax, Gray. Despite the kiss on your doorstep, I didn't come here for that."

He nodded, stepped to the bar, and made himself a drink. He took a sip and sat down across from her. "What's up?"

"Speaking of weekend plans, I'm surprised you're not staked out somewhere keeping an eye on your ex after what happened to her."

"She's got Marissa, and I have deputies doing a drive-by of the house every so often."

She went silent for a moment and then continued. "Her return has got me thinking about this case. Jeremy Barrett had an excellent defense planned, although he was doomed from the start. He couldn't get rid of her confession, and she was adamant that she was guilty, and every piece of evidence in that case proved she was guilty. But there was always something missing."

"A motive," he finished.

She looked directly at him. "And a body. If you had been conscious during that time, you probably would know the motive."

"What are you saying?"

She put her drink down and leaned forward in her chair. "It's always been the one thing that irked me, you, and the rest of the town. She would never say why she did it. Her own lawyer couldn't get a reason out of her, and he tried hardest of all to get her to talk since it could've saved her from a sentence."

"I'll ask you again," he said. "Where is this all leading?"

"Maybe you weren't supposed to survive that car accident."

Gray put his glass down slowly and shook his head. "I'm afraid to guess at this, but I get the feeling you're about to tell me Shannon is trying to kill me."

"It's the only explanation that gives me a motive," Gretchen said.

"Which is...?"

"Money, of course. The oldest reason in the book."

He shook his head. "Shannon's not interested in money."

She gaped at him as though he'd grown a second head. "I know you grew up privileged and maybe a little sheltered, but I refuse to believe you're that naïve."

"I know her."

"She shot your brother, but probably didn't need to shoot you because you were pretty much dead already. She would have access to the family fortune, and who would dispute it?"

"What about the fact that someone broke into and vandalized her house, and that she was attacked a few days ago?"

She shrugged. "Staged for your benefit. I know this may be a bruise to your ego, but maybe she was setting herself up for a hefty payday."

He didn't say anything more, not wanting to admit to her that he'd tossed the idea around in his head when he'd first been released from the hospital and was desperately trying to recall the events of that night. But he'd immediately dismissed the idea because he didn't want to believe that about Shannon. Still, in the back of his mind, there always lurked the feeling that he had been somehow targeted by her, and the moment she walked into the sheriff's station that night, soaking wet from the rain, it had been a deliberate move on her part.

"Gray, did you hear me?"

He snapped his focus back to Gretchen. "What?"

"I asked if anything has come back to you about that night."

He shook his head. "Snatches of conversation between Shannon and me. My voice is always raised, so I get the feeling I'm angry with her about something. But I can't get any details. I do remember rain. Heavy rain."

"And Cody?"

His gaze automatically drifted to the framed picture of him, Cody, and their parents during Cody's college graduation. It had been the last family picture taken before his parents were killed in the car crash.

"That's the one thing that bothers the hell out of me," he replied, feeling himself drift deeper into thought.

"What?"

Gray frowned, focusing on his brother's beaming smile in his royal blue cap and gown with a gold tassel. "If I buy your theory or any other theory for that matter, it doesn't explain Cody."

He then looked up at Gretchen. "What was he doing up there?"

CHAPTER NINETEEN

Five years ago…

"What's the matter?"

"Nothing," I said and then shrugged. "I just don't understand why you're coming to me. Why not go directly to Gray?"

Cody and I were leaning up against his car as we observed the construction crew stand together in a circle and stretch, ready to begin the morning's work.

"You're family now, so I'm going to include you in a little family drama. I've never been very good with finances—not like Gray. My brother has grown impatient with me coming to him for money, and it's already starting to put a strain on our relationship. I don't want this to damage it any further."

I held the takeout coffee cup in my hands, absorbing Cody's words and feeling very uncomfortable. This was the second time the two of us were meeting to discuss something that would affect Gray without Gray himself being present.

"Listen," Cody said, turning to me. "You two have inspired me. I want to turn my life around. I've found a great career and a place in the city that won't charge me out the ass for rent. I'll be able to take care of myself, but I want to start out with a clean slate. This money will help with that by getting rid of some old debts."

I was still feeling uneasy about the whole thing but figured it would be the best way to repay a favor. Cody, after all, had given me the courage to pursue Gray, and that had gotten me here: married and surprisingly happy.

"How would we do it without Gray knowing?"

Cody's smile was triumphant, and I noticed it was the same smile I'd seen the night he convinced me to walk into the sheriff's station soaking wet from the rain.

"Let me handle the details. I'll contact you later this week." He turned, reached inside the open window of his car, and pulled out a medium-sized velvet box.

"Congratulations," he said, handing it to me.

I looked at the box and then at him in a silent question.

"Open it later if you want," he said, leaning over to kiss me on the cheek and then walking to the driver's side of his car. He paused, looked at the house, and then back at me.

"You did well for yourself, Shannon. It's a shame your aunt couldn't be here to see it."

I smiled uneasily, not liking the look in his eyes. Maybe I was reading too much into his words, but the subtle meaning behind them was all too clear. I watched him drive away, and it wasn't until his car was farther down the street that I lifted the lid of the box. White gold gleamed back at me in the form of earrings, a tennis bracelet, and a necklace. All three pieces were inlaid with diamonds and my birthstone, rubies. I looked up in the direction of his car, but he was completely out of sight. Frowning at the expensive jewelry, I couldn't help the sickening feeling that I'd just been paid off.

CHAPTER TWENTY

*I*t hurt to come back here, but I should be used to putting myself in painful situations by now.

I edged my car over to the side of the road and switched off the ignition. For a moment, I simply sat there, staring up at what used to be my house—my and Gray's house. I thought immediately of our honeymoon night and how he'd waited before I nearly drifted off to sleep before casually announcing he had a wedding present for me.

Not just any wedding present, but a house, and not just any house, but this house, the one in complete ruin that sat atop a hill overlooking the lake. The state it had been in had turned away many prospective buyers, but I'd made it my goal to purchase it for myself someday and make a home for Aunt Christine and me. Then Gray had come along, blew my mind, and just like that, it was mine.

Tears came to my eyes just as they had that night he'd handed me the deed and the keys, along with the memory that my aunt wasn't there to see it, and that I hadn't deserved any of it. In the next instant, I wiped the tears away furiously, thoroughly sick of crying over the past, especially when the circumstances were all my doing and based on the selfish choices I'd made.

I got out of the car and walked slowly to the front steps of the house. The breeze carrying in off the lake whipped around me, flirting with the skirt of my dress.

When we'd returned to Gypsy Bay after a short honeymoon, I'd spent most of my days here, interested in the progress and overall transformation of something once considered ugly into something beautiful. I'd decided to keep the original style of the home, which was a two-story farmhouse. The existence of the wraparound porch and huge picture windows indicated the new owners decided the same thing. I wondered who owned it now and if they loved it as much as Gray and I had once.

The sound of an approaching car halted my steps. I whirled around and saw the sheriff's SUV coming up the road. When he got out of the car, I asked myself if there would one day come a time when he wouldn't affect me so strongly.

"Good morning, Sheriff," I said, eyeing him as he came toward me.

"You shouldn't be out here alone," Gray said in response.

"It's been a week since that bastard attacked me. I'm not going to start being afraid to go outside."

He just stared at me, and I hated how hard it was to look at him. Those brown eyes of his gave me the uneasy feeling he could see straight through to my mind. Even now, I felt like I had to explain myself when I hadn't done anything wrong.

"It's been a long time, and I wanted to see the house. How did you know where to find me?"

"You told me you were staying with Marissa for the time being. When I stopped by, she said you went for a drive. I followed a hunch that you might be here."

We stared at each other, neither of us wanting to admit just how well he knew me.

He looked down at the ground and then back up, his voice now firm. "I came to take you in, Shannon."

"Excuse me?"

He didn't repeat it. He didn't really have to.

"What's happened?" I asked.

"There's been another murder."

I faced the dawning sun, shook my head, and then glared at him. "So, you're arresting me?"

"It's just for questioning."

"So, question me. Right here."

"It needs to be in an official capacity."

"An official capacity? Don't talk to me like a sheriff. Talk to me like—"

"Like who? Your husband?" He came forward, ready for a fight. "No, I'm sorry Shannon, I can't do that because I'm not your husband. I'm the sheriff of this town, and I'm taking you to the station to be questioned."

"Gray…"

"Get in the car. I'll drive you myself."

I looked back toward the house, as though it might give me some form of comfort as it stood tall and silent against the lake. I then faced him, reading and understanding the look in his eyes that he was not leaving here without me. Squaring my shoulders, I strode past him, unlocked my car door, and retrieved my purse from inside. After locking it again, I followed him to his sheriff's vehicle, allowed him to open the door for me, and climbed inside. As we drove away, I gave the house one last wistful look.

"Don't worry about your car. It'll be safe here," Gray said, misreading the longing on my face.

I kept my view on the house as it got smaller in the side mirror until it was finally out of sight.

"Whoever you sold it to loves it very much."

I was still staring out the side mirror but sensed him turning to face me.

"You can tell by the finishings and details on the exterior. Things I didn't think about when—"

"You have the right to have an attorney present," he said, cutting off any further trips down memory lane.

CHAPTER TWENTY-ONE

Gray sat beside Deputy Leah Collins in the interrogation room, trying not to look directly at Shannon. Leah would be taking charge of the questioning, for obvious reasons, but it didn't mean Gray had to like it. The three of them sat in silence as they waited for Shannon's attorney. She'd already been offered something to drink, which she refused, and there was nothing else to do now but wait in what was turning out to be an awkward situation. Usually, Gray would have waited in his office until her attorney arrived, but there was a need inside of him to keep close by her at all times. He pretended to be studying notes inside a file, all the while sending furtive glances her way when he was sure she wasn't looking. He noticed the way her eyes moved around slowly, observing every detail in the room and how she kept her hands laced together only lightly, not tense at all. He looked to her left hand and finger, where her engagement ring used to be. He remembered the day he'd removed his ring. The tan line had stayed there for months. It was now faded as if it had never been there.

It had been on the tip of his tongue to tell her the house

still belonged to her—to them—but that would have led to more questions he didn't know how to answer. Questions like: *Why did he keep the old house? What did he plan to do with it when the renovation was complete?* Those kinds of questions would only cause him to look at the past and ask himself if he was ready to let go of it all and everything that reminded him of her.

His eyes slid over to her again, and not for the first time, he noticed she was wearing that red and white polka dot number he'd always loved, showing off her brown toned legs and full thighs that he imagined straddling him. She was never one to wear dresses a lot, but when she did, it was always a treat for him. But the fact that she could stir something up inside him also angered the hell out of him. Yes, it was definitely a good idea to conduct this questioning in official surroundings.

The door to the interrogation room swung open, and Gray looked up to see ADA Gretchen Miller stride in with Jeremy Barrett, Shannon's attorney, right behind her. The sight of Jeremy always made Gray's gut clench. He never had anything against the man. He was a great defense attorney, and Gray often wondered why he wasted his time in a small town like Gypsy Bay when he could be making tons of money in a bigger city like San Francisco or even Los Angeles. He'd been Shannon's attorney when she was convicted of manslaughter three years ago. He'd been told, however, Jeremy couldn't do much for her, because she'd been so adamant about confessing to the crime, and pleading guilty. He'd been told the man had fought to the bitter end for Shannon, which made Gray wonder, not for the first time, if his loyalties ran deeper than the professional level.

The two of them had grown up together, attending the same public schools, while Gray and Cody attended the more elite private schools in the area. Gray didn't resent his stellar education, only that it cost him the opportunity to share the same memories as Shannon and Jeremy. Even now, they sat together comfortably, sharing a smile filled with memories that only old friends would know about. Gray had his hands underneath the table, only to hide them from sight as he clenched them tightly.

Leah cleared her throat. "Okay, now that we're all here, I'd like to commence the interview—"

"Hold on a minute, Deputy," Jeremy interrupted, "I want a moment to talk to my client."

They all started to rise, but Shannon spoke up. "There's no need, Jeremy. I didn't do anything."

He put a hand over hers, leaned over, and whispered something in her ear. The too-close contact caused Gray's blood to begin to rise.

Shannon pulled away and seemed to be warring with herself and whatever he'd just told her. Then her eyes found Gray, and the stark worry in them slammed into him. Gray rose from his chair before he did something stupid like go to her and wrap her in his arms until that fear was gone.

"We can give you five minutes."

That seemed to propel everyone into action. Once he, Leah, and Gretchen had all filed out, he closed the door and turned on the two of them.

"This had better pan out because if we go in there and begin accusing her of two murders with no proof, it's going to start to look like harassment."

Gretchen rolled her eyes. "Both murders were committed on her nights off, Gray, and beside each body is a piece of jewelry with her DNA on it, given to her by Cody."

"Her whereabouts can be explained, and the jewelry could have been planted."

"By whom?" Leah asked.

"By someone who wants to commit murder and has found an easy scapegoat."

Gretchen stepped up to him, speaking in that low casual voice she always used to get witnesses on the stand to soften up toward her. "Our job is simply to get answers. That's all we're doing. She's a big girl, Gray. Let her explain herself."

He didn't like the subtle warning in those words for him to back off because, after this interrogation, there was no doubt in his mind she'd be calling up the mayor to give him a full report of everything that went down, including his performance.

He looked through the window pane of the door and noticed Jeremy waving them back inside.

"Let's get this over with," he muttered.

Gray, Leah, and Gretchen all stepped back into the room, and the women resumed their seats. Gray, however, chose to remain standing. Leah went through the routine of announcing the start of the interview and the names of all who were present. She then confirmed with Shannon that she had been made aware of her rights and began the interview.

Leah started the interview by holding up the plastic evidence bag with the bracelet inside.

"Ms. Spencer, do you recognize this piece of jewelry?"

Shannon shot a look at Gray and then back to the evidence bag. "It's mine."

"Where did you get it?"

"Cody Spencer gave it to me five years ago, shortly after Sheriff Spencer and I were married. It was a wedding gift."

Leah put the bag down and held up a similar one, only this one had the ruby earrings inside. Deputy Collins slid the bag across the table to Shannon.

"What about these? Were these a gift from Cody too?"

Shannon sighed heavily, and Gray wished he could tell what she was thinking.

"Yes, they were."

"Each piece of jewelry was found clutched in our two victim's hands. Your DNA is all over them. Can you tell me how that would happen?"

Jeremy put a restraining hand over Shannon's. "Don't answer that." Then he addressed Leah. "Deputy, she already told you they belong to her. If she wore them, her DNA would be on them."

"Well, if they belonged to her, maybe she can tell me how they were found clutched in both Frank Miles's and Jason Hadley's dead hands."

"No, she can't," Jeremy said at the same exact time Shannon said, "Because I lost them."

Leah honed in on Shannon's answer, just as Jeremy began to object. "You lost them, Ms. Spencer?"

"Shannon—"

"Yes, I did," Shannon replied, cutting Jeremy off.

"How?"

She cast another look to Gray, who kept his arms crossed and waited for her to reveal everything that happened that evening.

"I don't know," she said, shrugging. "They weren't in my things when I moved back into my aunt's home. The house has been locked up for nearly four years, but someone could have found a way to get inside. Just like they found a way to vandalize my home and attack me."

Jeremy sat back, visibly relaxed. Shannon's explanation had left too much room for doubt in anybody's mind. They would have a hard time in court proving she'd had access to that jewelry when she'd been in Chowchilla for three years.

Gray, however, was seething. What was she up to?

Deputy Collins, apparently realizing she'd been defeated

in this part of the questioning, took back the evidence bag and started on a new subject.

"That brings me to another point. You say your home was vandalized. Someone painted the word *Murderer* in red paint over your walls and tacked up Cody's picture, correct?"

"Yes," Shannon said.

"Why didn't you report this vandalism to the sheriff's office the night it happened?"

"I figured it was a just a bunch of kids. Rumors about me are everywhere, and I was sure it was just some teenagers who wanted to be a part of it all. I've changed my locks since then."

"Then how do you suppose your attacker got in? There was no sign of a break-in, and you'd just purchased new door and window locks."

"I don't know," Shannon said, shrugging.

Deputy Collins paused before delivering a blow. "You didn't let him in, did you?"

"No!"

"That's ridiculous," Jeremy said. "Shannon, don't say any more."

Leah continued on doggedly. "Ms. Spencer, can you account for your whereabouts on May twenty-seventh around nine p.m.?"

Shannon seemed to take a few deep breaths in order to calm herself from that last outburst and focus on the deputy's next question.

"Ms. Spencer, do you need a minute?" Leah asked.

"I was sitting in my car outside Sheriff Spencer's home on Dearborn Drive."

Gray started. He pushed away from the wall, effectively discarding his seemingly composed stance and strode to Shannon. "What?"

"Sheriff," Leah warned, but she had seemed just as thrown

by the answer as he was. She shot him another look to back down and continued with her questioning.

"Why were you outside Sheriff Spencer's house?"

"Since I returned to Gypsy Bay, I've been keeping an eye on the sheriff."

Gray noticed how, unlike a few moments ago, she made it a point to keep her eyes on Leah and not look anywhere in his direction.

"I think someone is trying to harm him."

Gretchen scoffed, and Leah shot her a warning look as well.

"Have you seen or heard anything that would make you believe the sheriff was in danger?"

Shannon sighed. "No. Nothing."

"What about that night?"

She shook her head. "Nothing." She slid a look to Gretchen. "ADA Miller came by that evening, and I figured everything was fine, so I left."

Gray came forward again, ignoring Leah's exasperation. "What did you see?"

"Sheriff, if you'll allow me to ask the questions—" Leah started.

"What did you see?" Gray asked again.

Shannon slowly looked up at him. "I saw ADA Miller's white Mercedes pull into your driveway. She got out, rang the doorbell, and you answered."

Gray stared hard. "Then what?"

Shannon went silent, but he could see the anger forming in her eyes. "I saw the two of you kiss. Then you let her in and shut the door."

* * *

"I want to talk to her alone," Gray demanded.

"Not going to happen," Jeremy said coolly.

They had halted the interview and left the interrogation room after Shannon finished detailing her alibi. Now, Gray, Leah, Gretchen, and Jeremy were in his office strategizing over how to proceed with their witness.

"She just admitted to following me only to protect me," he said, trying his best to keep a lid on his temper because none of this was making any sense to him. "I want answers."

"And you're only going to get them if I'm in that room with her," Jeremy countered. "The last time Shannon spoke to a cop without an attorney present, she was sentenced to three years for manslaughter. I'm not letting that happen again."

Gray saw red. "You think that's what I want, for her to go to prison?"

"I don't care what you want. My job is to protect my client, and I don't care if she's holding the answers to the Kennedy assassination, she's not talking to anyone without a lawyer."

Gray didn't like how protective the man seemed to be over Shannon. He knew Jeremy was only doing his job, but damn! The thought of another man looking after her made him want to throw something.

"It's not a crime for her to keep an eye on you, Sheriff. I'll admit it's strange, but not a crime. She wasn't trespassing." He then divided a look between Gray and Gretchen. "Is what she said in there accurate?"

Gray didn't answer but shot a look toward Gretchen, who shrank under his gaze. She sighed and spoke up. "I did visit Sheriff Spencer that night, and there was a car several feet from his house that didn't look to belong to any of his neighbors."

"That must have been Shannon," Jeremy concluded. "What time was this?"

"A little after nine," Gretchen said. "And, yes, I did give the sheriff a very, very friendly hello."

Jeremy looked back and forth between the two of them, then to Deputy Collins who had lowered her head respectfully, and then he chuckled.

"Something funny, Barrett?" Gray asked.

"Look, Sheriff, you and I both know Shannon's not the gossiping type. She's not going to repeat anything she saw. Now, if you're feeling guilty because your ex-wife saw you with another woman, then work that stuff out on your own time. The point is, she was nowhere near that campsite at the time of the murder."

"Then prove it, counselor," Gretchen cut in. "I couldn't say for sure it was her sitting outside his home."

"She just described what she saw, right down to the make and model of your car, what you were wearing, and what happened in the doorway," Jeremy countered. "You two just corroborated that, and the medical examiner confirmed the victim's time of death as about the same time Shannon was in your neighborhood, Sheriff. My client and I are leaving."

CHAPTER TWENTY-TWO

*A*fter we left the station, Jeremy drove me to pick up my car at the old lake house. I then thanked him for his help, and we both got in our cars, heading in opposite directions.

I returned to Marissa's and was grateful for the fact that she was picking up an extra shift at the diner this evening. I needed a night to myself to figure out just what I was doing and what I hoped to accomplish.

I hadn't meant to admit the reason I'd started spying on Gray, especially after I'd made it plain I didn't want him protecting me. But as much as Gray was gung-ho on finding the man who'd attacked me, I had a sinking feeling he hadn't come there to kill me. Every punch and kick I'd endured had only been a message.

The doorbell sounded, and I nearly screamed, and then realized that instead of relaxing, I'd only managed to scare myself. I walked to the window and peeped out through the curtains. Gray was standing outside waiting patiently. Moving to the door, I sighed as I undid the locks and bolt, knowing this wasn't going to be a friendly visit.

I opened the door, and for a moment, we both stood there appraising one another, no doubt sharing thoughts of what was said during my questioning.

I spoke first. "You shouldn't be here."

"Well, I am here."

"If you want to talk, Gray, I can call Jeremy."

"This is between us. I don't need your knight in shining armor around."

"Stop it. You've got no reason to be jealous of him. You never have." I stepped away from the door as he entered and closed it behind him. Immediately, he towered over me.

He gave me a knowing look. "I guess I can't help it. Ever since that day—"

"You really want to bring that up?" I asked.

"No, but you could have."

"It wasn't relevant. I was there to prove I didn't murder that man, not that you're a jealous maniac."

He shrugged. "It wouldn't matter. I was the last one to have that jewelry. I even took it with me after we screwed our brains out that evening."

I swallowed, trying to keep the memories at bay and continuing to back away from him. "Why are you here, Gray?"

He began stalking my footsteps. "Why didn't you say anything? You could've taken the suspicion off of you and put it on me."

"Is that what you want me to do?"

"Yeah, it is," he said, raising his voice. "That would have made a lot of sense after you saw..."

He stopped abruptly and trailed off, looking embarrassed.

"After I saw you and Gretchen together."

His eyes remained steady. "It never went past that kiss."

"I don't care."

I started to turn away from him, but he hooked an arm around my elbow, jerking me back.

"Yes, you do. You care just like I do whenever Superman Attorney puts his hands on you. I know he's just comforting you. I even know it's all innocent, but it still drives me fucking crazy."

"If that's all you came to tell me—"

"It started a few months after our divorce," he continued. "It didn't last long."

"Jesus, Gray," I said, yanking my arm loose from his grip. "Why do you think I need to hear this?"

"Because I know you're wondering, and you have every right to know. Every wife does."

"I'm not your wife," I said, coldly echoing his words from earlier this afternoon. I turned my back to him, strode to the mantel, and then whirled back around, my eyes filled with rage. "And, yes, if it pleases your ego, I did wonder, but then I realized you have a right to a personal life, and even if it drives me crazy, too, it's none of my business."

He went completely still. "Where's Marissa?"

"She's working tonight."

"Then come here."

It had been years since I heard him use that tone with me. Even now, I was powerless to resist it. I moved from the mantel and stepped slowly toward him with my head held high in defiance. When I was within inches of him, he reached out, snaked his arm around my waist, and pulled me up against him. His other hand went to my ponytail and wrapped it slowly around his fist. He tugged gently at it, causing me to look up at him, directly into his eyes.

"What drove you crazy?"

"That kiss."

"Why?" he asked, keeping a firm grip on my hair, daring me to look away from him.

"Kissing a woman like that meant you'd had sex with her."

"How would you know that?"

"Because you would kiss me like that. Once that door closed, I wondered if you were putting your hands down her pants like you would do to me. I knew she'd be wet just like I would be. I knew that next, you'd stroke those fingers of yours like you used to do to me, watching and waiting for me to scream."

"Goddamn," he hissed and attacked my lips. His tongue fought and explored inside my mouth until I couldn't breathe. He then tore his lips from mine, whirled me around, and brought me up against the nearest wall.

"Spread your legs," he commanded.

I was still wearing the red and white polka dot sundress I'd had on that afternoon, and Gray knelt before me, reached up under the dress, and pulled my panties down. He looked up at me as I placed one hand on his shoulder and stepped out of them. Our looks of amazement that we were doing this mirrored each other's but neither one of us wanted to be the one to stop it.

"Hang on to me," he growled and moved his mouth to my ready and waiting pussy as if he belonged there. He feasted on me, feeling my body begin to move and react in the most natural way. I gripped his shoulders, my nails biting deep as I moved myself against his mouth, so every nerve had access to his quivering tongue.

"Gray, oh, God. Please!"

He was relentless. The faster he tasted, the faster I moved until we were in sync, each trying to outdo the other, but both going for the same outcome. I threw one leg over his shoulder, giving him further access until I was practically climbing him, desperate for pleasure. But he knew my body and what I needed. He gripped my full hips tightly, immobilizing me, and kept his tongue flickering rapidly against the tiny nub of my pussy. I stiffened, screamed and cursed him, slammed my head back against the wall, and came in a flood that was so satisfying and familiar.

* * *

I was dizzy with relief. I had so much pent-up sexual desire from the last four years that masturbation hadn't helped alleviate. I'd started using my vibrator again, but that wasn't enough either, even though every time I used the sex toy I became aroused by all the memories it conjured up of Gray sitting in the armchair of the bedroom and watching me use it on myself. But none of it: masturbation, sex toys, or memories had been enough to calm my appetite for Gray, except Gray himself, but the only thing I looked to be getting out of him tonight was his amazing tongue.

I huddled against the wall, feeling awkward as hell, as he reached down, picked up my panties, and handed them to me. Then he stood to his full height, and my eyes immediately went to the bulge in his pants. I looked up at him, and he was staring right back at me.

"I need to go," he said and headed for the door.

I stood. "If you're going to regret this in the morning, then save us both the trouble and just say it."

He paused with one hand on the doorknob, and I saw his back stiffen in anger. Later, I'd think this was pretty damn funny that I was having an argument with my ex-husband about oral sex with my panties balled up in my hand. Now, however, all I felt was humiliation, and I hated the next thought that floated in my mind. Where was he going to relieve that hard-on?

"We've got a lot of issues between us, Shannon. Sex isn't going to make them go away."

He turned and faced me, and when I saw the defeated look in his eyes, I suddenly felt foolish.

"In one night, I lost two people I loved, and I don't even know why."

With that, he turned, opened the door, and closed it behind him. I walked up to the closed door, locked it, and pounded my head softly against the frame.

"You do know why," I said to no one. "You just can't remember."

CHAPTER TWENTY-THREE

$\mathcal{T}$hree years ago...

When the guard came to the cell that afternoon to announce I had a visitor, I wanted to tell him to go to hell. I woke up that morning in a bad mood, and my day had only gotten worse. At lunch, I helped a fellow inmate out of a fight and had gotten my left rib punched for it. Needless to say, I just wanted to lie in my cell, nursing my injuries, not entertain one of Jeremy's appeal process visits.

When I went into the visitor area and saw Gray sitting on the other side of the glass partition, I stopped suddenly, causing the guard to bump into me from behind. I had to catch myself from smiling and running toward the partition. The last time I'd seen him, he was lying in the hospital bed, so still and peaceful. The deputies had given me the respect as the sheriff's wife to allow me to see him and speak to his doctor about his progress before handing me over to state authorities. Now, here he was, alive and mobile, and my eyes stung with relief that he was okay and that he'd survived the nightmare.

Gray's emotions also seemed to be warring, because he looked to be torn between whether to look at me as if I were his enemy or take me into his arms.

"What happened to you?" he asked, as soon as I sat down and picked up the phone to speak to him.

"You shouldn't have come."

"What happened to you?"

I realized then that I'd been reflexively holding my bruised side. "I got into a fight."

I could detect the exact movement of the lines on his face as he decided whether he should hate me or rip this jail apart and take me away. We hadn't been married long, but I knew my husband well enough and made the choice easier for him.

"I know why you're here, Gray, and you're not going to get any answers from me. Do you hear me? I shot Cody, and the only reason I'm not in here for murder is that they can't find his body."

His posture turned rigid, and I knew he was trying to keep himself together. "I know what you did. I'm here to find out why."

"You want a motive?"

"Yes."

I hated myself for what I had to do. It took every ounce of me not to tell him how glad I was to see him conscious. I wanted to tell him how much I missed him, but I needed him to stop searching for answers.

"I told you not to trust me. Do you remember that? The rainy night you took me home and let me drive your truck? I told you then, don't trust me."

"Shannon," he said, leaning forward. "Just tell me what happened. I don't know if you know this, but I lost my memory of that night. I don't remember anything. I've been trying hard to remember. I'm even seeing a psychiatrist to help me, but nothing is working. You know what happened, and I need you to tell me."

I sighed. "The doctors told me everything. I know about the memory loss, and it's just as well. I shot Cody. That's the end of it. Now, let it go."

His patience vanished instantly. "Are you fucking kidding me? You tell me to let go of the fact that my wife shot my brother, possibly killed him, and is now serving time for manslaughter? You think I want to see you in here?"

"It's where I belong."

"Goddamn you," he hissed. "Tell me what the hell happened."

I leaned back in my chair, still holding the phone to my ear, and studied him. He narrowed his eyes as if preparing himself for a blow. I needed him to forget me, forget Cody, and forget the ugly past. So, I delivered the blow without flinching.

"I married you for your money, Gray. That's all. There was nothing else between us, so I need you to get up, walk out that door, and leave me alone." I then leaned forward and got my face as close as I could to the partition. "As far as you're concerned, I'm dead, just like your brother."

He smacked the window with his open palm so hard that I jumped back, momentarily stunned. I knew the guard was coming up behind me, alerted by the noise, but Gray ignored him. His light brown eyes now hard and clouded over with grief, and I knew without a doubt he was experiencing what it felt like to love and hate someone at the same time.

"I don't know what you're trying to do here, but for as long as I live, I'll never believe you could be that cold-blooded."

"Then you're a fool."

For a long time, we regarded each other, squared off as if on a battlefield, waiting for the other to strike. I, however, grew weary of watching the man I loved look at me as if he didn't know me. So, like the loser in battle, I retreated. I hung up the phone, rose from my seat, and signaled to the guard I was ready to return to my cell. I didn't look back to see if Gray was still there. I wasn't going to risk him seeing the tears that filled my eyes.

CHAPTER TWENTY-FOUR

"*D*ammit!"

Gray pounded a fist on the steering wheel. He should never have touched her. That was the stupidest thing he could have done, but he needed for her to know and feel just how much he wanted her, how much power she had over him. Still, what had it accomplished? In the end, Cody was still dead, Shannon was still his murderer, and Gray was heading home both restless for her and confused more than ever.

He had to admit to himself that some of it had been guilt. Divorced or not, he never wanted her to see him kissing another woman, just as much as he would never want to see her with another man. When she'd confessed to seeing him with Gretchen, he wanted to explain everything to her right then and there, but it hadn't been the right time.

He would never admit to anyone but himself that he always wanted Shannon and would always want her. Maybe that was crazy, but it was the truth. His brief affair with Gretchen had been a way to prove to himself that he could move on with his life without her, but that hadn't worked out. Gray wanted his wife, guilty or not, and that made him feel pathetic because despite her orgasm this evening, he wasn't certain if she wanted him.

The porch lights of the large family home came into view, and that old feeling of despair started to creep back in. Suddenly, he didn't want to face that empty house alone, and he hadn't felt that way since he woke up in the hospital and found out his wife was imprisoned for manslaughter. In the days and months following, Gray remembered throwing himself into work until the point of exhaustion, with most nights ending with him sleeping on the couch in the break area of the station. He'd started leaving his uniforms and shaving gear at work, not wanting any excuse to return home. His staff began to suspect what was going on and some had even been brave enough to suggest he seek professional help. He had seen Dr. Kessler in hopes of unlocking his memory of what happened that night, especially since Shannon had remained silent each time he visited her in Chowchilla, but just like her, his memory had remained stubbornly closed.

He'd kept up the routine for a year: work, avoid the house, visit Shannon, see a psychiatrist, and repeat until one day he was just too damned tired of it all and called his lawyer.

He remembered pouring himself coffee in his office when Mike walked in with an unreadable expression.

Gray turned to him, coffee pot and mug frozen in midair. "Did you see her?"

Mike placed his briefcase on the edge of Gray's desk and rested a hand on top of it. "Yes."

"And did she—" Gray halted, just as he saw the tiny flicker of sympathy in the man's eyes.

He put the coffee pot and mug down and then went to his desk to sit down. He braced his elbows on the desk and rubbed his fingers into the sockets of his eyes. As he did this, he heard the briefcase open, papers shuffling, and then something sliding across the desk to him. Gray dropped his hands and looked down. The divorce papers he'd had Mike draw up two weeks ago were in front of him. The packet was flipped to the last page, and Shannon's signature was staring up at him.

"Did she say anything?"

He looked up and saw the older man shake his head. "She signed it and had the officer take her away. I'm sorry, Gray."

Gray said nothing but looked down and saw that his signature line was still blank. He'd left it that way purposely, as a last-ditch attempt to show his wife he didn't want to divorce her. He'd entertained fantasies of Mike calling him to say she'd ripped the entire thing into pieces or even a collect call from her cursing and screaming at him to say how dare he send her divorce papers, and that she refused to sign. He wanted to see if she was still willing to fight for them, to work this out, to tell him everything about that night because he still refused to believe she shot his brother in cold blood. But she hadn't said or done any of that. Nothing came back to him but her signature and silence.

You win, Shannon.

Gray grabbed a pen from the holder and viciously signed his name. He mumbled something to his lawyer that might have been thank you and left the station for the remainder of the day. He returned home, no longer feeling sadness about her absence. He welcomed the quiet. She'd made it perfectly clear what she wanted, and it sure as hell wasn't him. He opened and slammed the front door closed behind him, pretending not to notice the echo it made along the empty hallways. He went into his den, grabbed a glass and decanter of scotch, and went into the large open living area. He turned the TV to some mindless talk show, simply for the white noise it provided. Sitting down on the couch, he promptly poured himself a glass and drank it down in one gulp. That continued late into the night until he finally passed out from blessed numbness.

Gray shoved the memory back to the recesses of his mind as he pulled into the driveway of his home and got out. He let himself inside and went straight to bed. He hadn't been asleep for an hour when the smell woke him. The smell of burning.

CHAPTER TWENTY-FIVE

When Marissa came home that evening from work, she knew something was wrong. Shannon's car wasn't in the driveway, which was strange enough on its own. She checked the clock on her dash, which read ten minutes to one. What was Shannon doing driving around at one in the morning?

Maybe she wasn't driving around at one in the morning, a little voice echoed. Maybe she was safely ensconced in someone's bed. Gray's bed?

Marissa sighed and got out of the car, trudging her way up the porch steps. As she let herself inside the small bungalow home, she told herself Shannon was a grown woman and perfectly capable of making her own decisions. Still, it was hard to not interfere in her friend's personal life.

Shannon had left a light on in the living room, and Marissa mentally thanked her for that. Ever since that attack on Shannon, it seemed that everyone in the town was a bit jumpy, and most neighborhoods had started establishing a neighborhood watch program and the habit of keeping on porch lights. Together with the street lights, her neighborhood alone looked as if Christmas had come early.

Marissa dropped her keys on the side table by the sofa and immediately saw the note scribbled on a yellow legal pad.

Went for a drive. Gray came by. Need to clear my head. Love, Shannon.

She'd had the foresight to write the time, and it had been nearly two hours ago. Marissa sighed, removing her jacket and tossing it on the couch. She headed into the kitchen for a glass of juice and wondered what Gray could have said or done to make Shannon restless. The diner had been crazy busy tonight, so Marissa didn't have time to call her and ask how her interview at the station went. Apparently, it must not have been too bad because they didn't arrest her. She supposed thanks should go to the sexy criminal attorney, Jeremy Barrett. Marissa smiled to herself, wishing she could be a fly on the wall in that interview room. It was no secret that Gray was not a fan of Jeremy simply because Jeremy was smart, successful, tempted most women into committing a crime just for his representation, and he seemed to have a soft spot for Shannon.

She would bet every last tip she made this week that Gray came by to remind Shannon that he was the only man allowed to consume her thoughts. Marissa winced. Gray and Shannon were sexy as hell together, but she didn't want to be a fly on that wall. That was more of her friend than she needed to see.

Her thoughts came to an abrupt halt when she heard the front door open and close softly. She looked to the kitchen doorway but only saw a shadow moving along the wall of the living room. She stepped to the entryway.

The glass of juice fell from her hands and crashed to the

floor. She backed up against the counter, steadying herself and slightly laughing.

"You scared the shit out of me! I got your message, but I didn't think I'd see you at all tonight."

* * *

He smelled smoke. Gray sat straight up in bed, quickly trying to orient himself, and looked to the closed door of his bedroom. When his parents had been alive, they'd fallen into the habit of always leaving a faint hallway light on at night for the boys. It was mainly for Cody, who'd grown up suffering from nightmares and tended to run into their parents' room during the middle of the night. The tradition had continued well after Gray and Cody had grown up and left for college. After their deaths, Gray had moved into the family home and didn't see a need to stop the tradition either.

He was glad for that fact now because as he peered down at the crack between the closed door and the floor, he saw a shadow moving. Then there was the faint sound of a key sliding into the old lock.

Gray threw back the covers and leaped out of bed. He grabbed the firearm he left in a nightstand drawer and crossed to the bedroom door. He turned the knob but knew before he tried that it would be locked. He kicked at it over and over, hoping to crack the hinges, but it was solid oak. He put his ear to the door and listened as running footsteps faded down the hallway.

Damn!

Suddenly, the smoke alarm sounded from somewhere downstairs, possibly the kitchen. Gray hurried back to the nightstand and reached for his cell phone. He dialed 911 and was immediately patched through to his dispatch operator.

He recognized the woman's voice on the other end of the line.

"Arlene, it's Sheriff Spencer. Send the fire department and deputies to my house right away. I'm locked in my bedroom, and a fire has been started somewhere downstairs."

Arlene wasted no time in gathering all the necessary information. She was professional as always, but Gray couldn't mistake the surprise and fear in her tone, no matter how well she masked it.

"Fire department personnel are on their way, Sheriff. The deputies in that area should be reaching you shortly."

Gray hung up the phone and grabbed for a pair of pants and T-shirt flung over an armchair. He donned them quickly along with a pair of sneakers. He crossed to one of the three windows of the bedroom, opened it, and looked down. It was at least a twenty-foot drop.

The smoke alarms were sounding all throughout the downstairs now, and there was no mistaking the smell now. Soon, he would be assaulted by the fire and the smoke. He needed to get out.

He hurried to the adjoining bathroom, snatched one of the hand towels off the rack, and drenched it under the faucet. He would have to risk heading downstairs. There was no telling where the fire was, but if he didn't get out fast, he'd quickly run out of exits.

He ran out of the bathroom and crossed the room to the door. He cautiously felt the knob, which was still cool to the touch. He didn't hesitate, stood back, and shot at the lock twice. He flung the door open and charged down the stairs. Smoke swarmed the house, blinding him. He began coughing uncontrollably but kept the wet towel to his nostrils. A quick assessment told him the kitchen was engulfed in flames, but he knew his home like the back of his hand and felt his way toward the foyer and what should be the front door.

Gray cursed a blue streak inside his head. There was so much smoke enveloping the entire first floor that he couldn't see a damn thing. His eyes were watery and stinging from the smoke, and he could feel his lungs beginning to burn. He knew the dangers of smoke inhalation enough to know that he was running out of time, but he kept reaching out with one hand while keeping the towel against his face with the other. Where was the front door? He began to feel along the walls for the nearest window. His den had to be close since it was situated right off the foyer, but Gray had become disoriented. Still, he turned to his left and entered what had to be his office.

A hand clutched around his wrist, and he reflexively started to defend himself, not sure if this was the person who started the fire and somehow got trapped inside.

"Gray, don't! It's me."

Shannon.

"I broke open a window; come on!"

She put an arm around his waist, and they both ducked low as she led him to the lone window of his office. He shouted at her to go first, shoved her up by her butt, and pushed her through the window. When she was through, he climbed up on the frame, ignoring the glass shards cutting through the palms of his hands, and pulled his way out.

He then grabbed her by the hand, and the two of them ran to the front of the house, away from the smoke and flames. Gray's lungs burned with the feel of clean oxygen hitting them. He bent forward, bracing his hands on his knees, and coughed up as much as he could. He felt Shannon's hand rubbing his back, soothing him with words of encouragement. When he felt the coughing subside, he slowly rose to his full height and watched as the rear of his house went up in flames. He then looked to the woman standing beside him, and for the first time, wondered what she was doing there.

She faced him too and seemed to read the question in his eyes.

"I said this afternoon I believed you were in danger. I couldn't sleep and wanted to make sure everything was okay here. Then I saw the flames."

"You came by to check on me."

She gestured an impatient hand to his burning house. "It's good a thing I did. Someone wants you dead."

They heard the first sound of sirens. Shannon looked in the direction of the sound and suddenly became nervous. Gray didn't take his eyes off her.

"It seems to me everything that's been happening around here started as soon as you got back to town."

She sighed. "That's what he wants you to think."

"He? Who's he?"

She started to edge away from him. "I have to go."

He grabbed for her hand and clutched it. "You're not going anywhere. My deputies are going to want a statement from you. I'm curious to hear your entire story too."

She wrenched her hand free. "It's not a story!"

The sirens were growing louder and closer, and with them, Shannon's agitation seemed to rise to full-blown panic.

Gray frowned. "What's the matter?"

The gun came up so fast. Gray hadn't even been aware she was carrying one. "Drop your gun and get down on the ground."

He was stunned. "What is this?"

"Drop your gun!"

He hesitated for just an instant and then tossed it at her feet. "Shannon, talk to me, baby. What's going on?"

"I don't have time to explain. I asked you to get down on the ground."

"You're not going to shoot me," he said, using the tone that made so many suspects and witnesses feel relaxed in his presence. "You didn't help me get out of a burning house only to kill me on my lawn."

"Get down!" She pointed to the ground with the gun and Gray obeyed, slowly lowering to his knees and then lying face down.

"I didn't hurt her, Gray."

"What?"

But she was running away. He heard her sneakered steps running across the street and climbing into her car. Gray lifted his head as the fire trucks roared down his street, the sirens now at a deafening pitch. Shannon's car disappeared in the opposite direction.

CHAPTER TWENTY-SIX

Gray sat inside an ambulance, obediently breathing into a nasal cannula. He didn't need the oxygen, but it had been the only way to keep the EMTs from fussing over him. He looked through the open door of the vehicle and noticed his neighbors staring in fascination as nearly every emergency vehicle in Gypsy Bay surrounded his damaged home.

Through the army of deputies, he noticed Leah Collins coming his way. Since she'd relocated here, she'd proven herself to be an able deputy. He was glad he'd made the decision to take her under his wing, but now with the disapproving frown she wore, he wished she'd turn and walk the other way.

"You didn't see who it was?" she asked as a way of introduction.

He shook his head, removing the cannula. "They locked the bedroom door with one of those old skeleton keys and ran off."

Leah gaped. "You have those kinds of doors in that house? Those old doors that can be locked from the outside?"

Gray shrugged. "It's an old house. It belonged to my grandparents."

"That old house nearly killed you tonight."

"Whoever started the fire nearly killed me."

Leah sighed. "Okay, so you didn't see who it was? Any ideas?"

"No."

"Well, we've got a lead, and your ADA friend is over there on the phone with Judge Stevens, demanding he sign an arrest warrant for Shannon Spencer."

Gray's head snapped around, looking for Gretchen. Christ. "What arrest warrant? On what grounds?"

"We responded to a nine-one-one call an hour and a half before yours. It was Marissa's house. Neighbors say they heard a lot of screaming and things crashing against the wall. When the deputies got there, the place was a mess, and there was no sign of either Marissa or Shannon. The manager at Charlie's said Marissa left as soon as they locked up. Marissa's car is still there, but Shannon's car is missing. A lot of blood was found in the kitchen. Its type matches Marissa's.

"We have an eyewitness who recognized Shannon's car. Apparently, one of your neighbors keeps a constant vigil of the street and wrote down her license plate each time she rode by the neighborhood. He says tonight he saw the same car driving away just before he heard sirens. It was the same plate, make, and model."

Gray rubbed the back of his neck, not liking the picture that was forming before his eyes.

I didn't hurt her, Gray.

"There's something else, Sheriff." Leah called to one of the other deputies, and he came forward to hand her a plastic evidence bag. "They found this on the grounds. The suspect must have run out of time and decided to drop it, but it was in plain enough sight."

When she tried to hand it to him, Gray simply shook his head, already knowing what it was with the way the moonlight reflected off the diamond and ruby necklace. The final piece of the jewelry set had been found at what should have been a homicide.

Leah handed the evidence bag to the other deputy, who walked away. She stepped closer to Gray and leaned forward to give them a modicum of privacy.

"I know you two have a history—"

"If she's trying to kill me, then who beat her up?" he asked, cutting her off.

Leah stared. Maybe it was out of respect for him or for Shannon because she had once been his wife, but she didn't say out loud what he knew she was thinking. They were both law enforcement officers, and whether it was the big city or a small town, they'd both grown cynical after seeing what people could do to each other. Shannon could have hired someone to attack her or any number of possibilities. Gretchen's theory was sounding more logical to him with each passing day. If Shannon married him for his money, she would need to get rid of both brothers. Was he really supposed to have died that night on the cliff?

He looked up at his deputy and could tell she was waiting for his response. She knew she had the evidence, but she still wouldn't make a move without his consent.

"Put an APB out for Shannon's car. Find her and arrest her."

Leah nodded, and Gray looked away from the pity in her eyes and instead focused on the flashing red and blue lights of the emergency vehicles.

CHAPTER TWENTY-SEVEN

"Sheriff, I haven't seen you in a while. How have you been?"

Gray gave Dr. Brian Kessler a handshake and polite nod before sitting down in the visitor's chair. The psychologist's office was located in a casita to the side of his home. Gray had never been much for seeing a counselor, but he had to admit Dr. Kessler had a way of putting him at ease. He should have continued seeing him, but it was Gray's own impatience with himself and miniscule results he was getting from his memory that brought the sessions to an end. Now, given the circumstances, he felt he needed some help.

"You said I'd slowly begin to get my memory back from that night," Gray said, coming straight to the point.

"Have you?" Brian asked, taking the seat behind his desk.

"There's just one conversation that keeps playing over and over like a loop. I'm arguing with my wife, I mean ex-wife, about money. We're driving, and it's raining."

"I understand. What do you need from me?"

Gray shrugged. "Do you have any suggestions, maybe exercises I could try to help speed things along?"

Brian frowned. "I don't want you rushing this, Sheriff. The mind has a way of remembering on its own. It will come back to you. If it wants to."

"What do you mean by that?"

"There may be a reason why you don't want to remember that night. Maybe your mind feels you can't handle it."

Gray bent his head, growing frustrated. "Look, you've heard by now Shannon is back, and since her return, things have been happening around Gypsy Bay."

"You think she's responsible?"

"I haven't decided yet, but I can't help but believe whatever is happening around here has something to do with the night…"

"The night you went into a coma."

"I think I may have seen something or heard something, I don't know, but it could be the key to all of this."

"Sheriff—"

Gray erupted, slamming his hand on the desk. "I've been patient for four damn years!"

"Gray," Brian said, firmly. "The mind isn't something to be forced. Now, if you want, you can keep revisiting the scene of the accident, and it may or may not help. Something as small and simple as a word or sound might bring it all back."

He stood, rounded the desk, and leaned against the corner. "I'm going to tell you like I told Mrs. Spencer; you need to be prepared for the fact that your memory of that event may not come back at all."

Gray had started to tune his words out when he wasn't getting the answers he needed, and then, just that quick, he had his attention again.

"Mrs. Spencer?"

Brian looked sheepish. "Sorry. She was Mrs. Spencer at the time I spoke to her."

"When was that?"

"Nearly four years ago. You had been in a coma for two weeks, and she was escorted in by your deputies, wanting to know how you were progressing. She was very upset, afraid you'd suffered fatal injuries, maybe brain damage, but I put her at ease."

He paused and looked to be recalling images from that day. "She took the news well when I told her that, aside from some memory loss, you should be in good health."

"You told her I would probably have memory loss?"

"Yes," he hesitated. "She was your wife at the time, Sheriff. She was entitled to know—"

"Never mind that," Gray cut in. "I'm not here about HIPAA violations. What did you tell her about the memory loss?"

He frowned, trying to remember. "I told her not to be surprised if you didn't remember much, if anything at all, about that night."

Gray's thoughts began to race, flooding him with a thousand possibilities of what this could all mean.

"What did she say?"

"Nothing. But it surprised me because most family members get upset when they hear these sorts of things about their loved ones. She didn't seem upset at all. She was just…"

"What?"

Brian frowned, and then he leveled his gaze directly on Gray. "Relieved."

CHAPTER TWENTY-EIGHT

"*It's not how it looks.*"

"*Then explain it to me, Shannon, because from what I'm seeing, you've been writing checks that range between five thousand to seven thousand dollars a month. It's not the contractor's fee because I spoke to him, and he told me his men have been paid. What the fuck is going on?*"

"*Slow down and stop yelling.*"

The memory came to him so clearly, as though it had always been there. Money. Why had they been arguing about money? He'd had the memory flash two days ago, and ever since, he'd been struggling to remember more. Still, he was now convinced that his memory was doing what it hadn't been able to do in four years. He was beginning to remember.

Gray wound the curve along the high cliffs that led to the northern point of Gypsy Bay. It was the same scenic drive many tourists took on their way through the town and into neighboring cities. He and Shannon were taking this drive that night on the way to a friend's house for dinner. He'd taken the drive several times alone over the past few years in an effort to jog his memory, but he always failed. He was hopeful this time, although it would probably help even more if Shannon was in the car with him, talking him through the events of that fateful night.

But Shannon was gone.

Two days since the fire and Marissa's disappearance, and they'd been unable to track her. She hadn't returned to work, to her aunt's home, or contacted anyone. He'd tried calling her cell phone, hoping that if she saw his name and number appear, she'd trust him enough to answer the call. All the while, Gretchen and her new best friend Mayor Porter were determined to see Shannon locked up with the key thrown away. With Shannon's sudden disappearing act without any explanation, her guilt was a certainty in everyone's minds. Gray, however, didn't know what to think, and it made him both furious and afraid.

He slowed to a stop when he came to one of many curves in the road separating the high cliffs and ocean by a metal rail. He switched off the ignition and got out, immediately assaulted by the salty sea air coming off the waves. He went over to the railing, braced his hands, and looked over. It was a steep way down to the water, but not too steep of an incline for him to make his way carefully down to the jagged rocks below.

The sound of thunder in the distance made him hesitate for just a moment. He looked up and saw storm clouds moving in from the east that would soon darken the entire sky. He would have to make this fast.

He put one leg over the railing, thankful he'd had the foresight to go home and change out of his uniform. Steadily, he moved down the hill until he came upon the rocks. He moved along as the waves splashed, sending water high and in several directions. Gray bent at the waist, peering between the rocks and grass, not exactly sure what he was looking for, only knowing that Cody must have fallen down this way and into the sea. Any evidence of his death would have been washed away years ago, but Gray just needed that one thing, anything, that could have been left behind.

Overhead, thunder sounded again, and drops of water fell to the back of his neck. That's when he sensed something behind him. With one movement, he reached for the gun at his side. With the next, he was aiming it at the shadow behind him.

The gun must have startled her because she backed away reflexively. She missed her footing and nearly tripped over the rocks. Gray snapped one hand out to steady her. He tucked his gun into the back of his waistband and gripped her with his other hand.

"What the hell are you up to?"

"Gray—" Shannon started.

"Did you kill her? Did you kill Marissa?"

"You know I didn't."

"What are you doing here?" he asked, shaking her.

"I'm—I'm sorry," she said.

"I came here to remember. You knew what I was trying to do," he said it like an accusation.

"Yes."

"Why? Why don't you want me to remember? What are you doing here?"

"I told you. Someone's trying to kill you."

"Bullshit!"

"It's true."

"Then, who? Who is it?"

He was in her face now, yelling and so full of rage. She'd followed him out here to this place, risked being arrested, all because she was so afraid of something he might remember.

"Who is it, Shannon?"

"Cody."

He tightened his grip on her arms. "You fucking liar."

"I'm not lying!"

"Cody's dead. You're saying a dead man is trying to kill me?"

"I know it's him."

"How? How in the world could it be him?"

Tears came to her eyes, but he didn't have the patience for them.

"Answer me!"

"Because he tried to kill you that night. That's why I shot him."

CHAPTER TWENTY-NINE

The sky opened up just as Gray ushered me up the hill, and the light drops turned to a heavy, pelting rain that drenched the two of us by the time we got to his car. He opened the door and practically tossed me inside before hurrying to the other side and climbing in. On the way to the house, he didn't speak or look at me. I, however, watched him constantly, waiting for him to react to what I'd said to him. But his silence had continued until we were inside the lake house. He'd unceremoniously tossed a blanket over my shoulders and told me not to move as he went through the house, closing the windows against the storm. When he returned to me, he was rubbing a towel against his damp hair and looked surprised to see me still standing in the foyer, wrapping the blanket around myself tighter.

"I thought you were taking me to the station."

He tossed the towel aside, pulled out a chair from the dining table, and gestured for me to sit down.

"I need answers from you first. Sit down."

I hesitated and then came slowly toward him. He kept a

steady gaze on me until I was sitting down and then grabbed a seat across from me.

"Where's my brother, Shannon?" he asked, getting straight to the point.

"I don't know."

"You said he's alive."

"I believe he is."

I didn't like the look on his face. He was at his limit of patience with me, and I would have to tread carefully if I was going to get him to listen to me without erupting.

"I know it sounds incredible, Gray, but hear me out, please, before making any judgment."

He leaned back in the chair and crossed his arms, his eyes never shifting away from me as I told him how Cody encouraged me from almost the beginning to pursue him.

"I thought he was just playing matchmaker," I said. "He talked you up, made you sound like some kind of superhero. I didn't think you'd ever be interested in a girl like me, but Cody kept my confidence up. He even suggested I go as far as showing up at the station in the rain."

Gray's jaw tensed, and I knew he was reliving that memory. He'd said it was the night he fell in love with me, and I instantly hated myself for taking a moment in time that had been so important to him and defiling it.

"After we were married, everything was going fine until Cody visited me here during construction. He asked me for money. He told me he was in a financial mess and didn't want to bother you with it. I felt sorry for him because he seemed to respect you but didn't want you disappointed in him. I agreed to loan him some money, and he asked me to take it from the construction account, so you didn't get suspicious."

Realization seemed to dawn in Gray's eyes.

"What is it?"

He hesitated and then asked, "You wrote him checks from that account?"

"Yes. Why?"

"Go on."

But I didn't want to go on, namely because the events only got worse from that point, and I wanted to address what had triggered such a reaction from him.

"This went on every month for the next six months until I finally just stopped. I felt like he was taking advantage of me, and I didn't want to lie to you anymore."

"How did he take it when you told him you were cutting him off?"

I shrugged. "At the time, he seemed okay with it. He even apologized for making me feel used and said it had not been his intention. I left him, thinking that would be the end of it, and felt a lot better." I paused and looked toward one of the many large picture windows and outside where the storm was in full uproar.

"Then the night came when I got a call to come to the hospital because you'd been shot."

* * *

"You're lucky the bullet went straight through the upper chest cavity without hitting any major arteries."

I listened with one ear as the doctor went over Gray's injuries and his recommendations for the following weeks as part of his healing process. The other part of me was on Cody, standing off to the side, playing the role of the concerned brother.

What have I done? What have I brought into Gray's life? When had this gone from a simple deal to attempted murder?

The thought of the bullet being just a few inches closer to Gray's heart made me suddenly feel nauseous.

"You're certain you didn't see anyone, Sheriff?"

One of his deputies had come to the hospital to take his statement as a matter of formality.

"No, nothing," Gray said, as the doctor began stitching him. "Listen, I'm thinking it may have been some kids who got ahold of their parents' gun and are too afraid to come forward."

"They could've killed you, Sheriff."

The room was beginning to spin. I practically fell into a chair beside the bed and dropped my head to my knees.

"Can we do this later?" I heard Gray addressing his deputy in lowered tones. Then Gray called to me. "Shannon?"

"Can I get you anything, Mrs. Spencer?" the doctor asked.

I raised my head and saw that everyone was now looking at me. "I just suddenly felt nauseous."

The doctor gave me a sympathetic smile. "He'll be fine. I know it's not every day you see your husband with a bullet wound, even in his line of work."

My eyes went to Gray, but I knew they could never convey just how sorry I was for everything.

"No, it isn't," I said.

"Cody," Gray said, "take Shannon to get a ginger ale or something. That will help with the queasiness."

"No," I rushed to say, feeling Cody coming to stand over me. "I'll be fine; I promise."

"Go," Gray said. "Let him stitch me up, and then we can go home."

"Come on, Shannon." Cody was grabbing me by the arm now. "You could use some air."

To anyone else, it looked to be gentle urging, but I could feel the bite in his grip. To avoid making a scene, I rose and allowed myself to be led away. When we left the private room and had made our way farther down the hall away from suspicion, I snatched my arm away and turned from him to hide the tears welling in my eyes. He grabbed my face and turned me to look at him. For a moment, he simply frowned at me, and then it turned into a grin, and finally, he began to laugh uncontrollably.

I jerked my head from his touch and just looked at him with all the hate and disgust I felt for him.

"Wow," Cody said when his laughter subsided. "The gold digger is in love."

"Go to hell."

"Maybe, but not until I get what's mine. Don't forget, beautiful, you signed up for this."

"I never signed up for murder."

He shook his head sadly. "You're the one who isn't cooperating. I told you what I wanted, and you stopped giving it to me."

"It isn't right, Cody."

"Where were your morals when he put that family heirloom on your finger?"

I stepped forward and put my face as close to his as I could get without biting him. "You can call me all the names you want if it makes you feel better. I don't care how you feel about me, but I do care about him."

"I believe you."

"Then you'll know I'm not bullshitting when I tell you this ends now. You try anything like this again, and I'll kill you."

I stepped away from that smirk, wrapped my sweater tightly around me, and walked off back to Gray.

* * *

When I finished talking, silence fell between us for a few moments. Then Gray leaned forward, lacing his fingers together.

"With all this going on, you never once came to me. Why?"

"There was no proof; I only had my signature on blank checks. They were never made out to Cody."

"You thought you needed proof for me to believe you?"

"I'm not naïve, Gray. Cody was your brother. You loved him. You would never have believed a word I said about him if I didn't bring you something."

"I also know my brother and his habits. If you had come to me, yes, I would have been angry, but I would have believed you."

"Even if I told you he wanted to kill you?"

He looked away from me and cursed.

"Of course not," I said, guessing at his thoughts. "No one would ever want to believe that of someone they loved and grew up with."

He started rubbing at his eyes and then abruptly stood and crossed the room to a large window that overlooked the side of the house, giving a partial view of the lake. I remembered how adamant I was in making sure we had a wraparound porch, providing a place to sit from every area of the house. I also felt a longing at seeing the French doors I'd wanted had been installed, providing easy access to the porch.

"What happened after I left you at Marissa's?"

I paused, eyeing him to see if that statement affected him as much as it did me. Did he immediately think about the encounter just as I did? It had rarely been far from my mind since it happened. I couldn't tell if it had been the same for Gray because he kept his vigil at the window, watching the storm rage outside while his emotions remained perfectly schooled.

"I tried going to bed, but I couldn't sleep, so I left Marissa a note and went for a long drive."

He turned to give me this look that said he was not in the mood for lies.

"It's the truth. When I came back to the house, it looked like she'd been fighting somebody. There was blood in the kitchen, and furniture had been knocked over. I looked for her all over the place, called her cell phone, but nothing. I got scared, so I ran."

"Why?"

"Why do you think? I knew you, your deputies, and Gretchen Miller couldn't wait to pin this one on me."

"Why didn't you just keep running?"

"Because Marissa is still missing."

"Marissa wouldn't be at the cliffs. Why were you there?"

I should have expected the question from a man as observant as Gray, but I hadn't, and as a result, I was blindsided. He pounced on my hesitation just like any cop would who sensed he was backing his witness into a corner.

"You had a few hours head start, and my deputies and I have been chasing our tails for nearly a week to find you. You could have left town altogether, but instead, you followed me up to those cliffs."

"Yes."

"Where have you been?"

"Holed up in some motel several miles from here. I used cash and checked in under an assumed name to give myself a chance to think. Marissa was missing, Cody was still out there somewhere, and I knew you were still in danger. I couldn't keep running if I wanted to. Cody committed those murders and probably even killed my best friend to frame me and get me out of the way. I'm the only one who knows what he tried to do to you, Gray. He wants me gone."

He returned his gaze to the window again, and this time didn't speak for a long time. I rose from the chair, clutched the blanket around me, and joined him by the window. Off to the right, the lake was rippling furiously from the high winds and heavy rain.

"What are you thinking?" I asked.

"I'm thinking you've just laid a lot on my plate. Cody was a lot of things, but a murderer?"

The anger was building inside me. I faced him, and when I spoke, I didn't recognize the steel in my voice as my own.

"You didn't find it hard to believe I could've killed those tourists. It wasn't too much of a stretch for you to think I could've killed Marissa."

His eyes flared when he faced me, and his tone was just as hard. "Cody isn't the one with a history of murder."

I stepped back, eyes wide. "But I just told you, he's—" I stopped, lowered my head, and shook it slowly. "You don't believe any of it."

His silence was more of an answer than I needed. I let out a scornful laugh. "And you wonder why I never came to you."

"Shannon—"

"Where's your phone?" I didn't wait for an answer but flung off the blanket and began going in and out of rooms, looking for a telephone or his cell.

Gray followed after me, dogging my heels. "Why do you need a phone?"

"To call Jeremy and tell him to meet me at the station. I'm turning myself in. You think I'm a killer? Fine. Let's get this whole mess over with."

"What you said that day, that first time I came to see you was true, wasn't it?"

I paused in my search for a phone and looked at him. "What?"

"You married me for my money."

He said it as though he already knew the answer but needed me to confirm it. "Yes. I liked and respected you, Gray, when we were first married, but I had other motives."

I supposed I could tell him that I'd been denying my affection for him for years and that I'd, in fact, loved him long before we were married, but the damage had been done, and I doubted he'd believe anything I said now.

"So, you knew I was crazy about you, and you decided to use that to play whore for me. Is that about right?"

I held my head up, despite the effect those words had on me. "I didn't want to lose my aunt, Gray. I wanted her to get the best treatments possible, but we were drowning in medical debt."

I heard myself saying the words but knew it sounded like a feeble excuse. At the time, the only thing on my mind had been to take care of Christine, to extend her life as long as I could. I had selfishly wanted to keep someone I loved in my life for as long as possible, even though they were suffering. As a result, I did a selfish thing by marrying a man without knowing what that commitment meant.

"And it was just bad luck for you when she died right before we were married. But you still stuck around, didn't you? I guess having access to half a billion dollars made that decision pretty easy."

Underneath the anger, I recognized the hurt and betrayal he must be feeling. But I didn't say anything, didn't try to defend myself anymore. I headed toward the front door, grabbing his keys from the console table. I would drive myself to the sheriff's station. Yes, he was upset, and I could understand the hurtful things coming out of his mouth, but it didn't mean I had to stand there and listen to them.

I made it all the way to the door but was halted as his hand gripped my upper arm. He turned me around to face him, but I immediately pushed him away.

"Dammit," I said, erupting from years of pent-up frustration. "Why didn't you just move on?"

"I didn't want to move on," he said. "I was married to you."

"You served me divorce papers."

"You left me no choice!"

We were yelling now, so Gray paused, ran a hand through his hair, and tried breathing in and out to calm down.

"I didn't think you loved me anymore, and when my lawyer came back to tell me you signed your name without a fucking argument, I didn't think you ever loved me."

I was shaking my head now, tears frozen in my eyes. "You should've got on with your life."

"Then maybe you should've stayed away. Why come back here at all? Why make me remember everything and even hope again?"

"Cody was—"

"I can handle Cody *if* he's alive. You should've just left me the hell alone!"

"Yes, I should have. I'm sorry."

He was warring with himself again, as though he didn't know what to do with me.

"This storm won't let up until later on tonight. Stay here in the guest room. I'll drive you to the station in the morning."

He walked off, leaving me in the darkened room with the lightning to illuminate that I was now alone.

CHAPTER THIRTY

*G*ray wanted so badly to throw something. The line between truth and lie was blurring with every word she spoke. Was Cody alive? Did his own brother want him dead? All he had was Shannon's word to go on, and how did he know she wasn't just trying to cover her ass by shifting the blame to a man presumed dead?

But if this were all truly some elaborate story she made up, he'd have to face the fact that he was in love with a cold-blooded killer, and that was something he just couldn't handle.

But someone had attacked her that night in her house, and someone had stolen that jewelry set and planted it on the victims' bodies. Someone had harmed Marissa and likely disposed of her body somewhere. Putting aside the point that he'd been married to the woman, he still couldn't see her doing those things. But if not her, then who the hell did it?

If he were to believe Shannon's story, it would mean that Cody had been holed up somewhere for four years, biding his time, knowing Shannon wouldn't be able to resist returning to Gypsy Bay. He'd killed two men and likely

Marissa to keep Gray distracted and put all suspicion on Shannon. Not to mention, someone had tried to kill Gray.

Was he ready to believe Cody hated him that much?

His thoughts drifted to random arguments he'd had with Cody and the hateful look he would sometimes see in his eyes. At the time, he dismissed it as temporary fury that would fade when Cody calmed down. There were other times he'd catch Cody staring at him with such raw anger it would concern Gray. However, before he had a chance to ask about it, Cody would mask it behind that charming smile so easily that Gray would be left wondering if he'd just imagined the whole thing.

He felt the first onset of a headache and put his hands to his forehead, wishing he could squeeze these disturbing thoughts right out of his mind.

* * *

It was nearly midnight, and the winds of the storm had calmed. Rain was left, and Gray was sitting outside on the porch, still wearing his clothes from that day, his gaze transfixed on something only he could see.

I quietly stepped outside through one of the French doors and made my way to him. My steps paused as I watched him lean down and clutch his head in his hands. I steeled myself, came forward and put the glass of water I'd been holding onto a small side table. The soft thud alarmed him as he sat up and glared at me. At the risk of being hypnotized by his piercing look, I thrust at him the pill bottle in my other hand.

"You should eat something, then take these. It'll help with the headache."

"I can handle it. Go back to bed."

I hesitated for a moment and then started to put the aspirin beside the glass of water. Gray's hand latched onto mine, trapping it underneath his and keeping me still. I kept my eyes on our hands for a long time before meeting his gaze.

"Was it all a lie or was it all about the money for you?"

"You wouldn't give up," I said quietly. "I never wanted you to know about Cody, so I said the one thing I knew would keep you away from me. But you kept coming back. You kept asking questions, so I stayed silent, hoping one day you would just give up."

His hand moved to my wrist and gripped it softly. "You lied to me."

"I wanted you to stop asking me the same questions over and over."

His grip tightened but only enough to make me drop the aspirin bottle.

"You lied to me," he said again.

"Yes, I lied to you."

With one tug, he pulled me onto the seat with him. In no time, he had my thighs straddling him, and it shocked and stirred me to be this close to him, so I immediately began to move away. Gray, however, guessed at my reaction and already had one arm held fast around my waist with his other hand holding the back of my head still, forcing me to look nowhere else but at him.

"That's a bad habit of yours," he said, his mouth barely moving. "Always has been."

"Gray, let me up," I said, continuing to struggle, but he only tightened his hold.

"I think you forgot who you married because I don't need you protecting me from anything or anyone, dead or alive. I'm a big boy, Shannon. I can handle the truth. I prefer the truth."

He removed his hand from the back of my head and moved it between our bodies. When his cool palm cupped me, I tried once again to move off him. Gray's strong arm around my waist pulled me back in even closer, putting more pressure between his palm and my pussy.

I moaned on pure instinct.

"Tell me the truth," he said, his eyes never moving from my face.

"What do you want me to say?" I breathed, my lower body moving against his hand to keep the pressure just right.

"Tell me how this feels."

"Good. So good."

"That wasn't so hard." He pulled my panties aside and put two fingers inside me. I cried out and immediately gripped his shoulders for balance.

"Why did you sign those papers?"

"I thought it was what you wanted."

"Wrong answer." He replaced his fingers with his calloused knuckles and moved them lightly against the tiny nub.

"I don't know, Gray. Please."

"Why did you sign them?"

I shook my head, feeling the tears well up from both the ecstasy of his touch and the memories of the past.

"I wanted you to move on from us."

He stilled his hands, but I kept up the rhythm of my body against the hard length beneath his pants. I felt his gaze steady on me as I writhed against him, my actions begging him to do what I couldn't form with words.

"Take off your shirt. I want to see the rest of you."

Through my haze of excitement, I unbuttoned the night-shirt I'd put on earlier and slipped it off my shoulders. I wasn't wearing a bra. I heard his breath catch ever so slightly at the sight of me and stopped moving against him to cover myself.

Gray halted my movements. "What are you doing?"

"They've grown bigger."

"I can see that."

"I gained weight while inside."

"I noticed that the first day I saw you again." He slipped his hands below my waist to cup my ass. "And I've fantasized about touching you ever since." He gestured to the shirt. "Let me see."

I hesitated and then let the shirt fall back down. Warily, I looked around, wondering if anyone was watching us through the rain.

"No one can see us. We don't have neighbors yet."

We. Maybe it was the fact that I hadn't been with this man in four years or the fact that being out here with him was so romantic. Or maybe it was just that one simple word that brought all the memories of our good times together flooding back. Whatever it was, when he covered my breasts with his wet mouth, and I felt the first sensation of his tongue teasing my nipples, there was nothing I could deny him. I clutched the back of his head, demanding him to take his fill, and he politely obliged with every suck, pull, and nip.

"Gray, I missed you."

He stopped, looked up at me with a question in his eyes I couldn't guess, and then bent his head to wrestle with the zipper of his jeans. I kept my eyes on him, questioning if he really wanted to do this with me. Yes, we'd indulged in foreplay since I returned, but did he really want to be inside of me?

When he freed himself, he wasted no time in lifting me by the waist and yanking my panties off. When I was astride him again, I was overwhelmed with the feeling of him. Nothing but him.

"It didn't work, Shannon." He plunged deeper inside, and I came alive. "You hear me? It didn't work. I can't move on from you."

He gripped the back of my head again and pulled me down to meet his lips for a kiss that left me gasping for air. I barely had enough energy to keep astride him, but Gray held me fast, setting the rhythm in a sensual dance I remembered from long ago. I tipped my head back and reveled in the feel of his touch, the sound of our moans mingling together with the constant fall of rain behind us.

"Jesus." Gray gritted his teeth and increased his movements to a pace that caused me to cry out from the orgasm tearing through me. Moments later, he came, his hands gripping me so tight it was almost unbearable and then finally his hands and the rest of his body went slack. I fell against him, and he leaned back into the chair, encircling his arms around my body. We stayed that way for a long time, listening to each other's heartbeats while the rain continued.

"Why didn't you sell this place?" I asked, my head resting against his shoulder.

"I couldn't."

"Why not?"

For a moment, I didn't think he was going to answer until he exhaled a deep breath.

"Because it's not my house."

I sat up to look at him, brushing my hair away from my face.

He shrugged. "It was a wedding gift, remember? When I bought this place, I put the deed in your name. You're the one who always wanted it, Shannon. It's always been your house."

CHAPTER THIRTY-ONE

I woke from a dreamless sleep, looked to the window, and saw the first light of day creeping over the mountains in the distance. The sun would be fully up soon, and Gray would need to take me into the sheriff's station. After we left the porch last night, we made a meal of cold sandwiches and then went to bed and made love again before falling asleep.

We hadn't talked about what would happen in the morning, but I knew he was a man of integrity, and even if his heart told him to protect me from the law, his sense of honor and duty would nag at his conscience.

I slipped from the bed, pulled on one of his T-shirts, and padded downstairs. I covered the entire area of the first floor until I came to a room that looked to be Gray's temporary home office. I crossed to the desk where a laptop and several files rested. One folder lay open with several colored photographs spread across the surface, and I instantly recognized them as photos taken of Marissa's house. My hand went to my mouth as I relived the scene I came upon that night through those photos. Blood spatter in the kitchen, chairs and a coffee table were overturned in her living room. Dishes lay smashed against the tile floor as if she'd been throwing them at someone to defend herself. Tears welled in my eyes as I thought about what she had to endure. I had been terrified that night I was attacked, but I'd been fortunate enough to escape any further harm. Marissa was missing, and no one knew why she'd been taken or if she was still alive.

I read the notes scrawled to the side of the photo of Marissa's door locks.

No sign of break-in.

Did this mean she had let her attacker in the house? Christ, no wonder Gray and everyone else suspected me. I'd been the only one with access to Marissa. She never spoke of a boyfriend, and as far as I knew, Marissa didn't have any family in the immediate area.

I flipped to another photo. This one pictured her personal belongings: her purse, cell phone, and car keys. Everything a woman would normally take with her had been left behind, meaning she'd gone against her will or had been carried out while unconscious. I started to move to the next photo when something stopped me. I studied Marissa's belongings again, paying very close attention to the key ring.

CHAPTER THIRTY-TWO

Five years ago…

If Gray had been forced to stay in the hospital overnight, I would have stayed with him. As it turned out, the doctor released him with the strict advice to get plenty of bed rest for the next few days, and I wasted no time in getting him out of there and away from Cody. The entire ride home, I said nothing, too disgusted with myself for putting Gray in this situation and debating whether or not I should tell him what I suspected. But how in the hell could I tell him that his brother wanted him dead?

Gray must have sensed my mood because he didn't try to engage me in any conversation. But when we walked into the house together, he turned to me.

"Let's go upstairs. I need to talk to you."

His look was so serious, his tone so firm, I feared maybe he already knew more than I'd thought. I followed behind him as he took tentative steps up the staircase. When we entered the master bedroom, he didn't say anything but removed the hospital scrubs they'd given him to replace his bloody clothes. He checked his bandage for leaking and put on his pajama pants. When he seemed to be struggling, I hurried toward him, but he put up one hand to stop me, and the look he gave me said to not come any closer. I slowly backed away, swallowed the hurt I felt and changed into my own pajamas.

I went into the adjoining bathroom, scrubbed my face, and tried not to stare into the mirror too long at my reflection. When I came out of the bathroom, dabbing my face with the hand towel, Gray was holding something in his hand. I tossed the hand towel onto an empty chair and then went to my side of the bed. When I noticed what he had, I went still. He tossed the black velvet jewel case on the bed, and it landed with a thud between us. I looked at it and then lifted my eyes to meet his and pretended that my heart wasn't racing.

"I told myself I wouldn't bring this up to you," he said, "but when the two of you walked out of my hospital room together, I couldn't let it go anymore."

"Gray—"

"I wasn't snooping. I had been looking for a pair of socks, and you know how sometimes they end up in your panty drawer."

I nodded. Before I moved in, my panty drawer had been Gray's sock drawer, and every so often, he'd toss a clean pair of socks in there out of habit. But he didn't need to explain any of this to me. I knew he would never spy on me or look through my things. It had been pure chance that he'd found that case, and it had been stupid of me to tuck such an expensive gift away like it was some kind of dirty secret. In hindsight, I should have just brought it home to him and said something like:

"Hey, look what your brother gave me as a wedding present? Big spender! Looks like you're going to have to take me somewhere real fancy to give me an excuse to wear them."

We would have had a good laugh about it, and that would have been the end of it. Now, by not telling him and hiding it, I made him suspicious of me.

"Just tell me," he said. "Don't make me ask."

"There's nothing between us."

He heaved out a breath that sounded as though he'd been holding it for a long time. He looked down at the velvet case, picked it up, and opened it. I could imagine the diamonds and rubies sparkling up at him.

He shook his head and let out a forced chuckle.

"Your birthstone." He then closed the lid firmly and put it on the nightstand by the bed.

"Cody can be very charming and generous. Not many women have been able to tell him no."

He stared at the case for a long time and then looked at me. "I don't want you ever to think you married the wrong man."

I should have said something. I should have reassured him, told him it was him I wanted, but it was because of me he was now clutching his left side in pain. I could tell him I married the right man, but then I'd have to tell him he married the wrong woman.

"I'd like to go to bed now," I said.

I ignored the disappointment in his eyes and climbed into bed. As soon as we were both nestled under the covers, he pulled me toward him and kissed me until I was panting for breath. Then he pulled my pajama shirt over my head and put his lips on my breasts. His actions were passionate but also deliberate, as if he were reminding me I was his wife, as if he were reminding himself. He turned me around so that my back was facing him, pulled down my panties, and entered me from behind. I was mindful of his injury but didn't object, allowing him to take my body. I couldn't deny him because I knew he needed this.

After we made love, the two of us fell into a deep sleep, or so I thought. At some time during the night, I felt the bed shift and opened my eyes and turned my head just in time to see Gray get out of bed. In my drowsy state, I saw him pick up the jewel case and leave the room with it.

"Gray, is everything all right?"

He turned around. "Go back to sleep."

It was all he said as he turned and left the room. I put my head back down on my pillow and closed my eyes, letting sleep take over again.

I rose early the next morning to make Gray breakfast, and as we sat at the table eating scrambled eggs, we both knew the jewelry was gone. Neither one of us spoke of it again.

CHAPTER THIRTY-THREE

When Gray awoke an hour ago to find that not only was Shannon gone, but so was his pickup truck, he'd been going non-stop. He'd rallied all his deputies into a conference room with a digital display of his vehicle on a screen moving north along the Pacific Coast Highway. He'd had a tracking device installed on both his sheriff's vehicle and his own years ago as a safety precaution and was glad to see it was paying off.

"This is the priority right now. I want to know anything you can tell me about this particular area," Gray said, gesturing to the map. "She's going there for a reason, and someone get me the file on Cody."

When he excused everyone, Gretchen, who had decided to crash the meeting, stepped up to him.

"This is ridiculous, Gray. She's making a run for it, and you're wasting time. Just go after her before she crosses state lines."

"She's not running," he said.

"You don't know that."

"I do. Her friend is missing. She's not going anywhere until she finds Marissa."

Gretchen frowned. "We have a warrant for her arrest because it's suspected she harmed Marissa. Now you're saying she's looking for her?"

"I don't have time to explain right now."

"Well, you better make time before I call the mayor, and you might want to start with explaining how she got your truck in the first place."

Gray gave her a hard stare. "If you want to go cry to Daddy, be my guest."

She stepped close to him with a disgusted look. "When I come back, it'll be with an affidavit to have you removed from this case."

She turned and stomped out of the conference room, nearly colliding with Jeremy. He followed her angry stride and whistled softly.

"Someone's pissed at you," he said.

"That's nothing new," Gray said. "Thanks for coming down."

Jeremy looked to the digital screen. "You're tracking her."

Gray simply nodded.

"Listen, Sheriff, why don't you let me follow her. I could convince her to come in and surrender peacefully—"

"I'm not trying to arrest her," Gray said, cutting him off. "I want to know where she's going and why."

Jeremy shrugged. "Why are you asking me?"

"Because, aside from Marissa, you're the only person in this town she was close to. The three of you grew up together. You know things about her that I never got a chance to find out. Shannon is looking for Marissa and… possibly someone else." He didn't have time to go into the supposed resurrection of Cody. "There's a reason she's heading this far north, and before I go after her, I want to know what I'm getting into."

Jeremy frowned and took another look at the digital screen. After a few moments, Gray saw realization dawn on his face.

"The cabin."

Gray pounced. "What cabin?"

Jeremy only seemed to become hypnotized by the blinking dot. "Marissa's parents own a cabin in Sierra Vista near Mount Shasta. She used to invite us and some of the other gang from high school up there for spring and summer breaks. It was all innocent fun, but I only went because…"

He paused, casting a quick look at Gray. "I only went because I knew Shannon would be there." He then shrugged sheepishly. "I always had this thing for her."

Gray could have told the man he'd suspected as much, but at this point, he really didn't care. He needed to steer this conversation back to the point.

"Do her parents still own it?"

"No. When they divorced years ago, they both agreed to give it to Marissa as part of the settlement. Her mother then moved to Washington. I think her father now lives in Texas."

Jeremy smiled as good memories seemed to take hold of him. "Marissa was always bragging about that place when we were in school. She was so proud of it. She even had a special key made for it. Red with white polka dots."

Gray froze for just an instant and then rummaged through the files on the conference table for the file on Marissa and the crime scene photos. He flipped to the one of her purse and car keys. The special key was missing. That's what must have tipped Shannon off to take his truck and drive into God knows what.

"How far is it from here?"

"About six hours. She should get there by the afternoon," Jeremy said.

"Write down the address, and I'll put it in the GPS," Gray said, as he grabbed for the keys to the SUV and his gun holster.

"I'll do better than that." Jeremy grabbed a pad of paper and pen. "I'll give you the shortcut. It'll save you about an hour and a half, and you just might beat her there. You'll be using back roads. Shannon won't use back roads. They remind her of—"

"Scary movies," Gray finished, shrugging on his holster and checking the clip.

Jeremy paused in the middle of jotting down directions and shot him a half-hearted smile.

"You know more about her than you think, Sheriff."

"Gray, I have Cody's file." Deputy Leah Collins stepped into the room and paused, seeing him with his holster on.

"Where are you going?"

"Where do you think?"

"Not alone, you're not."

"Give me about a half hour head start. If I don't go in alone, it may scare her off."

Leah spared a quick glance at Jeremy, who was still jotting down directions. "Can I speak to you alone for a minute?"

The moment they were outside the station, she got straight to the point. "Do you really think he could still be alive?"

He'd relayed the entire story to her that morning before the rest of his deputies began to arrive. He needed someone with an unbiased opinion to tell him whether or not he was chasing a ghost.

"I don't know. Shannon doesn't even know if he's alive, but she's convinced he is."

"Okay. For the sake of argument, let's say that when she shot him, somehow he survived. The truth still remains that she shot your brother with the intent to kill him, and all we have for motive is what she told you."

"You think she's lying."

"No," Leah said. "I don't think she's lying, and that's what scares me. If he is alive and is hiding out in that cabin, then she's heading up there to finish what she started that night on the highway."

CHAPTER THIRTY-FOUR

Four years ago...

I glanced over at the speedometer, watching it slowly creep up to 80 mph. I then warily looked at Gray with his stiff jaw and fingers gripped tight around the steering wheel. He was staring at the winding road ahead of us. The rain was coming down heavily, the huge drops sounding like cannons against the windshield. Gray, however, seemed not to notice and was taking the curves of the mountain as though it were a sunny day, and this was his own personal obstacle course.

"Maybe we should turn around," I ventured.

His eyes cast downward for just a second to look at the digital clock. "We'll make it," he gritted out.

I leaned forward in my seat to grab for the cell phone in my purse. "Give me the number to your friend's house. I'll call and tell them we're running a little late."

"I said, we'll make it."

I sat back, eyeing him. It had been the first time since we were married that he'd ever snapped at me like that.

"What's wrong?" I asked.

He stayed silent for a moment and seemed to be taking a few deep breaths to calm down.

"What are the blank checks for, Shannon?"

Suddenly, I wanted to slink away. I'd known this day was coming, and I'd known the only way I could get myself out of it was to tell him everything.

Damn you, Cody.

He'd forced me to keep sending him money but didn't give a damn what would happen if Gray found out.

"It's not how it looks. I can explain everything."

"Then explain it to me, Shannon, because from what I'm seeing, you've been writing checks that range between five thousand to seven thousand dollars a month. It's not the contractor's fee because I spoke to him, and he told me his men have been paid. What the fuck is going on?"

"Slow down and stop yelling."

His speed was increasing, along with my heart rate.

"Gray, please, slow down. In fact, I want to go home. I don't want to visit your friends if we're arguing."

"I want you to start talking. Are you stashing that money somewhere?"

"No."

"You're not spending it. Since we've been married, I can count on one hand how many shopping bags you've brought into the house."

I turned in my seat toward him. "I didn't have a choice. I wanted to stop, but then you got shot, and he said it was just a warning."

"What?" he asked, frowning as he turned to me. "What the hell are you talking about? What does me getting shot have to do with anything?"

"Gray, watch out!"

He faced forward and cursed as he swerved the car to the right, narrowly missing a deer. The car skidded uncontrollably along the slick roads and then plowed into the railing just over the cliffs. Out of the corner of my eye, I saw my husband's head slam against the side of the window. At impact, the airbags sprang out, and the two of us were plunged forward and back into our seats.

When the car came to a full stop, I looked around, trying to assimilate where we were. I looked down at myself but didn't see any blood. I then looked to Gray, who was unconscious. I reached over, felt for a pulse, and let out a silent prayer of thanks when I found one. Then I unlatched my seat belt and struggled to pull myself from the car. I winced as I noticed the crushed hood of the car slammed into the railing and then looked around, paying no mind as the rain continued its unrelenting downpour, completely drenching me in seconds. Darkness surrounded us, but through the raindrops, I heard the unmistakable sound of the waves crashing against the rocks far below the cliffs.

Turning back, I dropped to my knees beside the car and began to feel along the floor. I knew my body would be sore all over tomorrow, and I didn't know whether I had suffered any internal injuries, but I had to get to my cell phone and call an ambulance for Gray. Feeling about, I felt for any and everything that had been spilled and scattered from my purse at the impact of the crash.

Out of nowhere, headlights from a car slowly came up the hill toward the wreck. Without a thought, I abandoned my search for a phone, jumped up, kicked off my heels, and ran to the middle of the road, waving my arms to get whoever it was to stop. The driver came to a stop, turned off the engine, and when he got out, I felt a sliver of fear crawl up my spine.

"What are you doing here?" I shouted in order to be heard over the pounding drops. "Are you following us?"

Cody, dressed in a long raincoat, gave a half shrug. "Protecting my investment." He moved past me and leaned into the car to look at his brother. "Is he dead?"

"No, he isn't. Give me your cell phone, so I can call for help."

He straightened and came to stand directly in front of me. "I followed you two all the way from Gypsy Bay, and he was taking those curves kind of fast. That's not like Gray. He doesn't drive recklessly unless he's angry, especially not in this kind of weather. What were you two talking about?"

I wouldn't tell him anything. I needed to keep Gray safe, and if he suspected Gray knew anything about the blank checks, he might kill him right then and there.

"Were you talking about me?"

I only returned his stare.

He sighed with impatience. "Either you tell me, or I roll this car over the cliff."

When I still didn't speak, he started to reach into the car to pull the gear shift to neutral. I moved in to shove him away and blocked the car with my body.

"Don't you touch him."

Cody reacted so fast, fisting a hand into my hair and pulling until I cried out. Then he slapped me, and I fell to my knees on the wet asphalt.

CHAPTER THIRTY-FIVE

*L*eah only gave Gray a twenty-minute head start. By the time she had every available unit loaded up and ready to go, along with another set of directions provided by Jeremy, Gray's time limit was up.

"Everybody understands their orders," she called out, addressing her colleagues as they gathered around a parade of vehicles. "We go in quiet. I don't know what we'll find up there, but it is believed that Marissa Kyle is being held against her will. Find her and get her out safely. Shannon Spencer will also be there. It is not yet known what her role is in all of this, but you are to find her and detain her for questioning."

Several other deputies would remain to respond to any emergency calls around Gypsy Bay but had gathered to wish the others luck. Leah could feel the energy rising as everyone was getting amped up to go after their sheriff and possibly a murderer. It was a lot of excitement for a quiet coastal town.

"Let's move out!"

"Deputy Collins."

Leah turned and groaned inwardly as Gretchen marched her way through the vehicles toward her.

"Gray said you'd be back, and I don't have time for it right now. Any grievance you have against him, take it up with him when he gets back."

"Actually, I'm here to help. Gray may be biased, but he's not an idiot. I trust his instincts, so when I got back to my office, I stopped looking at his ex-wife and started digging into those she knew." Gretchen paused, reached into her messenger bag, and pulled out copies of official government documents to hand to Leah.

"What is this?"

"A marriage license," Gretchen said, arching an eyebrow. "Meet Marissa Kyle aka Marissa Spencer."

CHAPTER THIRTY-SIX

*D*usk had fallen by the time I made it to the Sierra Vista cabins. I parked Gray's truck about a quarter mile away and walked the rest of the way there. As a teenager, I remembered this place being filled with laughter, music, and the smell of barbecue during lazy summers. Now, it looked ominous and foreboding, but my gut was telling me Marissa was being held here, and Cody was not far away.

One hour into the trip, I was regretting not telling Gray. Maybe he would have understood if I'd mentioned the missing key, but there was a warrant for my arrest already, and there was no way he'd be able to let me go off somewhere Marissa *might* be. More likely, he would have locked me up and taken the trip himself, and I couldn't let that happen either. Not when I knew Cody was still alive and wanted nothing more than to see his brother dead.

Tourist season was coming to an end, so only a few cabins were lit and occupied. Marissa's cabin remained dark with no sign of life. I kept moving, crouching down low to the ground when I came to the windows so as not to alert anyone who might be lurking inside. From behind my back, I pulled out the gun Gray kept underneath his seat, and it wasn't lost on me that this was the same gun I'd been searching for that night, the same gun that should have killed Cody.

My heart was pounding so fast as I crept nearer to the back patio door, remembering Marissa's words from the diner. Had she had a chance to fix the lock? I backed myself against the wall outside and turned just slightly enough to peer inside. Nothing. No movement.

Holding my breath, I grasped the handle, and the door slid open soundlessly. I kept the gun down at my side and stepped inside to the small kitchen. The curtains were drawn, and with the sky slowly turning into night, I could hardly see a thing.

A small whimper came from the front of the house. My hand came up as I aimed the gun at the sound. Just as quickly, another hand came down, knocking the gun away. I didn't have time to cry out because my mouth was covered and I was pinned by a strong arm.

"Sshh," a voice hissed in my ear. "It's me."

Gray.

He must have felt my body relax against his because he let his hand drop from my mouth. He turned me to face him, and I nearly wept from the sight of him. In the fading light, I could see him motioning me to follow him into the living room. I nodded and waited for him to precede me. He bent down, picked up the gun I'd dropped, and handed it to me. I followed close behind him as we crept quietly to the front of the house. We entered the formal area, where all our school friends used to hang out and watch movies after stuffing ourselves with hot dogs and macaroni salad. In the center of all the ruckus and laughter had been Marissa. Only then, she wasn't tied to a chair, bruised, and bleeding.

"Marissa!"

Before I could go to her, Gray's arm shot out, holding me back. He looked toward Marissa, who was staring at us wide-eyed with tears staining her cheeks. He seemed to be silently asking her something, to which Marissa furiously shook her head. Satisfied, Gray stepped fully into the room.

"I'll untie her," he said. "You keep watch by the door."

I spared one last look at my friend to reassure myself she was okay and rushed to the front door. I peered out, and when I didn't see anyone, slowly opened it. I turned back to Gray who had ripped the duct tape from Marissa's mouth. She was full-out sobbing now, and Gray was doing his best to calm her with soothing words.

I whirled back around to the open door with my gun drawn, thinking I'd heard something. But there was nothing out there but mountains, trees, and the growing dark.

"We need to hurry," I said, turning back to them, suddenly feeling uneasy and uncertain why Marissa had been left alone with no one watching her. It all seemed too simple. Like a trap.

The realization slammed into me just as I saw Marissa's hand jerk up the moment Gray freed her. She shoved something against his neck, and I watched in horror as his body jerked and fell to the ground.

"What the hell are you doing?" I screamed.

Before I could rush to his prone body, I felt an electric surge that started at my lower back and spread to my entire body. I would have sagged to the floor, but an arm came around my waist, catching me in a firm grip.

"Hey, beautiful," Cody whispered into my ear. "I missed you."

I turned my head, feeling so weak, and met his gorgeous smile. He struck me with the Taser again, and I felt my entire body convulse one last time, and then nothing at all.

CHAPTER THIRTY-SEVEN

*F*our years ago...

I couldn't dwell on the pain. I started scrambling to my feet, but Cody grabbed for my hair again, twisting and yanking as he dragged me to the railing near the cliff.

"You can't stick to a plan, can you?" he asked, reaching down to pull at my wrist. I grabbed his hand and bit it hard until I tasted blood.

"Dammit," Cody yelled, freeing me.

I crawled away from him back to the car and blindly felt underneath Gray's seat. I knew he kept a gun underneath the driver's seat. I moved his lifeless legs out of the way and kept searching. No gun, and I was out of time and options because Cody came up behind me and lifted me by the waist. I fought him like a wildcat, clawing and screaming as he led me back to the cliff. I knew he was going to throw me over, and the last sight I would see before I plunged into the icy waters would be him, peering over the edge of the railing watching me die.

* * *

My eyelids felt so heavy, but I struggled to lift them anyway.

"Come on, sweetie, wake up. We've got a lot to do, and we're running out of time."

I recognized the voice of my friend. Marissa's voice. She was speaking to me in that comforting way that always made me feel as if I could count on her for anything. Only now it was laced with subtle anger. When I finally managed to open my eyes fully, I saw Gray's service weapon now aimed at my head. No, not a friend, but I'd have to cry about that later. To my side, I saw Gray, lying very still.

"He's alive," Marissa said, "but he's going to wake up soon, so I need you to get it together and get up."

I sat up, wincing at the aches pricking my body. "What's going on, Marissa? What are you doing?"

"Getting what should have been mine years ago."

I didn't bother masking the confusion I felt, and Marissa burst into joyous laughter.

"I almost forgot. He said I can wear it now since, after tonight, all this shit will be over with."

Keeping the gun on me, Marissa dug in her shirt for the chain around her neck. She pulled it out and yanked at the object it was holding. The diamond glistened as she pushed the ring onto her left finger. She then looked at me, a radiant smile on her face.

"I'm not a secret anymore. I'm Mrs. Cody Spencer."

I felt strong enough to rise to my knees, even though the news I'd just heard was enough to knock me over.

"You and Cody were married? When?"

"A month after you and Gray."

"Why?"

Marissa gave me a look as if I were the dumbest woman walking. "Money, honey. The same reason you married,

Gray, only I wasn't stupid enough to think I was in love with the man."

I then sighed and shook my head.

"I wanted so badly to tell you that you and I were sisters. It's a shame the two of you divorced."

I didn't know the woman standing before me. She looked and sounded like my friend, except my friend never sounded as bitter and angry as she did now.

"You've been helping Cody all this time," I said.

"I figured he was dead just like everyone else, and with Gray in a coma, and you getting arrested, I chose to keep quiet and see how things turned out. Then, three weeks after the accident, he showed up at my doorstep in the middle of the night. When he fell over that cliff, he broke his shoulder and cracked one of his ribs against the rocks before falling into the water. He told me he managed to pull himself out of the water and get away from the scene as far as he could before hitching to a neighboring town with a hospital."

I shook my head, trying to grasp everything Marissa was saying. I'd known in my gut that Cody hadn't died that night and was just biding his time until he could return to exact some sort of revenge. I just couldn't get my head around the fact that Marissa was helping him all this time and deceiving me.

"Those two tourists? The fire? That was all you?"

"No, it was Cody. I needed to keep an alibi, so on nights he made his little mischief, I was working."

"You were helping him frame me, Marissa. You wanted me to go back to prison?"

"You should be thanking me. Cody just wanted to shoot you in the head and be done with you. I told him this would get you out of the way just as easily." Marissa paused before continuing, and for just an instant, I saw the look of my friend. "Believe it or not, I didn't want you to die."

"But you—you just sat there," I began and blinked back the tears. "You just sat there and watched him pull me into the house and hurt me."

She took two steps until she was in my face and pressed the barrel of the gun against the side of my head. I closed my eyes to block out the fury I saw rising inside of her.

"Look at me!"

I hesitated and then opened my eyes, my head leaning to the side from the heavy weight of the gun.

"Don't you dare try to make me feel anything for you. You got to live in that big mansion with a man who loved you and no doubt fucked you to death anytime you wanted him, while I had to stay in that two-bedroom shack, working at Charlie's, waiting for Cody to inherit."

"After Gray was dead," I concluded.

"That's right."

Beside us, Gray began to moan. I only spared him a brief glance before facing Marissa again. I wanted her attention on me and not on Gray, who was too vulnerable at the moment.

"I came back to the house," I said. "It looked as if someone hurt you in there."

"Well, thank you," she smiled, sweetly. "I knew I did a convincing job. To tell you the truth, that wasn't supposed to happen so soon. But Cody came that night and said he didn't want to wait any longer. He was going to get rid of Gray, my body would look to have disappeared, and it would be back to Chowchilla for you."

I let the tears fall freely. "What have I ever done to you? Tell me! Tell me how I've hurt you so that you would even think about doing this to me."

She slowly lowered the gun and stepped away from me. "You have no idea what it's like to live in the shadow of someone else. From junior high until now, it has always been about you. Everyone loved you, especially the guys. From Jeremy to Gray…to Cody."

I shook my head in denial, but she only laughed.

"It's okay, sweetie. He likes to hide his feelings behind a tough exterior, but I've known for a long time how he feels about you." She paused to give me a wink. "A man doesn't give a girl rubies and diamonds if she doesn't mean anything to him. Oh, you can thank me for that little touch to each body. I found them among some of your things Gray had boxed up."

I had assumed he gave the jewelry set away, but it didn't matter right now. The door flew open, and Cody stepped inside the cabin. He looked to me and then turned his attention on Gray. Even now, after all these years, I saw nothing but indifference in his eyes for his brother. Marissa rose and rushed to speak, sensing Cody's impatience.

"He's coming around now."

"We'll have to make this fast," he said, glancing at his watch. "There's no way in hell he would have come all the way out here without letting his deputies know where to find him. Take her. I'll get him up."

I rose slowly to my feet as Marissa kept the gun trained on me. I watched as Cody turned Gray over with his hands bound in front of him.

Gray let out another groan and opened his eyes.

"Cody," he rasped.

"That's right. Get up, big brother."

Gray stared at him for the longest time, and I saw the briefest look of joy at seeing a loved one alive, and then anger clouded his eyes as he looked around and saw me.

"Let Shannon go," he said.

"Can't do that. She's part of the plan."

"Where are you taking us?" I asked.

"We have a nice spot picked out for the two of you.

Marissa was so sure you'd figure out where to find her. We've had it picked out for weeks."

I looked to Gray, who was on his feet now. We stared at each other, and I knew we had to be thinking the same thing. We'd been led out here to disappear.

CHAPTER THIRTY-EIGHT

*L*eah punched the accelerator as she and a train of sheriff's department vehicles raced to the Sierra Vista cabins.

"Why didn't any of this come up before?" she asked Gretchen, who refused to be left behind in Gypsy Bay.

"Because we weren't looking for it. Everyone assumed Cody was and would always remain a confirmed bachelor, and Marissa wasn't exactly going around announcing it to everyone."

"So, she marries Cody to help him carry out his plans and claim the inheritance."

Gretchen shook her head. "Something tells me Marissa is a short-term solution. Since he is presumed dead, she'll claim the inheritance as the only living relative. But once she does, what's stopping him from…"

Leah turned to her, her mind forming the same conclusion. "She's a liability."

Gretchen nodded. "If Cody would go this far to kill his own brother for money, what's one little secret wife to get rid of?"

"So, four years ago, Cody ambushes Shannon and Gray on the cliff, hoping to kill them both at the same time," Leah surmised. "But Shannon wasn't unconscious from the accident like Gray and shoots Cody first."

Gretchen didn't say anything, and Leah guessed she was busy wrestling with the scenario in her own head, trying to make the puzzle pieces fit.

"Something still doesn't sound right," Leah continued. "If Cody planned to kill Gray, and Shannon was only acting in self-defense when she shot him, why didn't she just say all of this? Why go to jail when she might have gotten off?"

"Cody is from a wealthy family," Gretchen said. "Who would believe that he was plotting all this time against his own brother? More likely, people would believe Shannon was plotting to make herself a very rich widow."

Leah shook her head, not buying it. "Gray remembers hearing her scream and then a gunshot."

Gretchen shrugged. "Makes sense. She was scared and shot him before he could shoot her."

But Leah was now muttering to herself. "A scream then a gunshot, a scream then a gunshot."

"And if you believe Mrs. Wicker's statement, it was a scream, a gunshot, and a gunshot."

Leah turned sharply. "What?"

"She's an older lady who lives nearby the scene. According to her statement, she heard Shannon scream, then a shot followed. That's when she called the police. But a few minutes later, she swore she heard another gunshot. I remember Jeremy wanted to call her in as a witness to trial because ballistics found two shell casings, but there didn't seem to be any use since there wasn't going to be a trial, and her statement didn't prove his client innocent."

Leah nodded, keeping pace with the sheriff's vehicles in front of her. "It must have been the second gunshot that

Deputy Caine heard when he came upon the scene. So, Shannon screamed, shot Cody who fell over the cliff, and a few minutes later, she shoots the same gun? Why? What or who was she shooting at?"

"Hopefully, you can ask her yourself," Gretchen said, looking straight ahead. "That's if Cody doesn't silence her first."

CHAPTER THIRTY-NINE

"I'll hand it to you, Gray. You married a very persistent woman."

They were standing several feet from the cabin around a freshly dug grave, deep enough to hold both Gray and Shannon.

Cody kept his gun trained on Gray while sending Shannon a wink. "I knew you wouldn't, so I took it upon myself to make sure she had a nice welcome home."

"By murdering innocent people," Gray said, not taking his eyes off Cody.

Cody sported a wounded look. "That was for you. Five years as sheriff, and you hadn't had one juicy case yet, except for my supposed death. Now, your ex-wife returns, and since people already believe she's capable of murder, I just kept it going." He turned the gun on Shannon. "Call it payback for interfering in my business."

Gray stepped forward, and Cody snapped the pistol back into his face. Gray didn't flinch but kept his voice even.

"She's got nothing to do with this. You want the money

that bad? Take every goddamned penny if you want. Just leave Shannon out of it."

Cody frowned in disgust. "Jesus, what is it with you? She married you for your money. She played your whore just to get in your pockets, and you're still defending her."

Out of the corner of his eye, he saw Shannon wrestling with the binds on her hands, struggling to get free. Marissa came up behind her, poking the gun into the small of her back to still her and called to Cody.

"We need to wrap this up."

But Cody didn't seem to hear her. "You tell me what it is about her that makes you so fucking loyal to her? Don't tell me her pussy's made of gold."

Gray's tone remained the same calm tenor. "She never tried to kill me."

Cody smiled, lowering the gun only slightly. "Touché. But then again, you left me no choice. You, Mom, and Dad always thought I was a fuck up, and you never wasted a moment to let me know it. Now, as an added humiliation, they die and leave you to dole out an allowance to me like I'm ten?"

"Spare me the tantrum," Gray said through gritted teeth. "I've had enough of your sob stories. Poor little rich kid."

Cody smirked and then motioned to the open grave. "Get in, and because I'm a reasonable person, I decided to let the two of you rot in the same ditch."

Gray turned to the grave, looked to Shannon, and hoped she saw the promise in his eyes that, however this ended, he'd make sure she would be all right. Then he turned back to Cody.

"I love you, Cody. But if I'd known how much of a rotten bastard you turned out to be, I'd have killed you myself that night."

The sudden change in Cody's demeanor startled Gray. The gleeful smile he wore turned ugly, and for the first time in his life, Gray witnessed the unmasked, raw hatred his brother had for him.

He moved so fast, Gray was caught off guard. Still, he could never have prepared for the feeling of the gun being whipped to the side of his head. The pain was so great, it caused his legs to buckle. He dropped to the ground on his knees, his hands still bound.

"Gray," Shannon cried.

Cody stood over him and leaned down. "How did that feel? Did that trigger your memory yet, big brother? No?"

Another blow to his skull knocked him over onto his side. He fought his way through it, determined not to black out.

"Cody, you son of a bitch, leave him alone!"

Gray heard Shannon's screams and wanted to yell at her to keep quiet. He wanted his brother's attention on him for as long as it took for his deputies to arrive. He felt his right arm being pulled and his body lifted to the kneeling position. Blood was trickling down the side of his head as Cody's face came into his line of vision.

"You piece of shit," Cody hissed. "Your gold-digging bitch of a wife didn't shoot me that night."

He sent a vicious kick to Gray's stomach, and he bent at the waist from the force of it, his face landing in the dirt. He turned his head to the side and met the same brown eyes as his in Cody's.

"You did."

Blood mixed with sweat trailed down Gray's face, nearly blinding him, but he saw enough as he continued to stare at a man he'd loved his entire life, and what stared back at him was nothing but the truth. It was the jolt his sleeping memory had needed to awaken. After four years, Gray remembered.

CHAPTER FORTY

Four years ago…

It was her screams that brought him back to consciousness, but everything was so hazy. He looked down and saw there was blood on his shirt and on the deflated airbag. His blood. What happened?

Shannon was screaming.

Gray forced his mind to focus. He peered through the windshield and saw she was fighting someone. It was a man, and he was dragging her like a ragdoll toward the railing. Gray grunted and cursed as he struggled to undo his seatbelt. He reached underneath his seat and felt for the gun he kept there.

Hurry, dammit. She needs you.

He was lifting her by the waist now, holding her so tight. Jesus, he was going to toss her over the cliff. Gray finally found the gun and gripped the handle with hands slick from blood. His body protested as he removed himself from the car. He put one hand on the hood for balance and raised the other to aim. His arm hurt like a son of a bitch, but he was going to shoot. Then the man's face was shown by the glare of the headlights.

Cody?

So many questions flew through his mind, but he didn't have time to entertain any of them. He was beginning to feel weak and faint. Any moment now, he was going to pass out, but he couldn't leave Shannon helpless. He would just wound his brother, just to get him to stop, and then ask questions later.

Shannon's right arm came up and knocked Cody's head back. His grip seemed to loosen, but not enough for her to get away.

"You stupid bitch," he growled.

Gray didn't know whom he was looking at. The rage on Cody's face was plain. He wanted to kill her. The thought slammed into his mind as he watched his brother rear back, ready to deliver a blow to the side of her face.

"Cody!"

His shout caused them both to stop, and Gray didn't hesitate. He fired one single shot and watched in horror as his brother released Shannon, flailed, and then screamed, falling over the side into the water.

God forgive me.

He looked to Shannon, dropped the gun from his hands, and coughed. The taste of blood filled his mouth. By the time she ran over to him, he'd collapsed to the ground and surrendered to the darkness, grateful to remember nothing.

* * *

I wept as I kissed the side of Gray's face. I looked around the deserted road but saw nothing but the lights of a few homes hidden far back into the trees. The gunshot would have alerted someone, so I only had minutes to do what I needed to do.

I used the hem of my dress to wipe the gun residue from Gray's hands. I then took the gun and fired one shot into the air to give my own hands the residue. I'd come into this marriage on false pretenses, nearly got him killed, and he ended up saving my pathetic life. I owed him this much.

A car was coming up the hill. I kept the gun clutched in my hands, not knowing if this was a friend or another enemy. When I saw it was a sheriff's department vehicle, I bent down and kissed Gray one last time.

"I love you," I whispered.

Then I ran out into the road and stood directly in front of the vehicle's headlights. I immediately recognized Deputy Caine when he got out, pointing his weapon straight at me.

"Drop the gun, Shannon!"

I could do this for Gray. I would do this.

"I can't find my cell phone. Please, call an ambulance."

ray's eyes moved to Shannon. Tears fell down her cheeks. He could read the apology in her eyes but refused to accept it.

"Get in," Cody commanded again, gesturing with his gun to the open grave. "Let's get this over with."

They all heard it at the same time and turned in the direction of the woods. The booted footsteps came from somewhere hidden in the trees but close enough to know they were out of time.

Gray, however, was the only one who didn't look. He'd been expecting the sound. He reacted instantly, headbutting Cody. The action left Cody dazed, and Gray took advantage by bending at the waist and plowing headfirst into his stomach.

From his peripheral glance, he saw Shannon use Marissa's momentarily stunned look to raise her bound hands and knock the gun away. Marissa cried out at the hit to her wrists, but Gray knew the gun had fallen from her grasp because the two of them dove for it. Gray had his hands around Cody's neck while, in the back of his mind, he worried for Shannon and prayed she'd get her hands on that gun first.

The steps around them grew louder as Gray kept his hold on Cody. Soon, they would be surrounded by his deputies. He just needed to buy more time. Then he heard a scream, and the fear that ripped through him at the thought of Shannon being hurt broke his focus long enough for Cody to punch at his side and stun him. Gray rolled to his side in agony, and Cody got to his feet, grabbing the gun that had fallen out of his grasp. Gray looked up to see the barrel aimed at his head.

"Let's see you keep what belongs to me now."

The rapid-fire shots plunged into Cody. He dropped the gun, stared down at the three holes in his chest, and looked to Gray, just before dropping to his knees. Gray sat up and struggled to catch him. Cody kept his eyes on him, and Gray tried to ingrain in his memory the look of his little brother again before Cody's eyes went lifeless. Gray held him as what sounded like an army of deputies crashed into the clearing with firearms drawn.

"Drop your weapon! Drop the gun!"

Gray looked up to see Shannon standing over him and Cody's body, gripping the gun tightly.

"I thought I heard you scream," he said.

"That was Marissa. I got ahold of the Taser." Shannon tossed the gun at his feet and raised her bound hands in surrender.

$\mathcal{I}$ sat in the sheriff's station, exhausted both mentally and physically. After I'd given my statement, I was asked to wait in the visitor's area. I hadn't realized I'd begun shivering until one of the deputies put a jacket around me. I thanked him but hardly noticed the chill due to my complete focus on Gray as he sat in his office surrounded by Gretchen Miller, Deputy Collins, and other law enforcement personnel. He was obviously giving his own statement, and I wished I could be in there with him but didn't dare ask.

At one point, he looked through the glass partition into the waiting area, and our eyes connected. But the look had been so fleeting, I almost thought I'd imagined it.

But I knew I hadn't imagined it. There was stark clarity in his eyes. Eyes that told me he remembered everything. I never wanted this to come out; I never wanted him to know, not like this. My plan had been to return to Gypsy Bay to make sure Gray would never know anything about that night. I would have been content for him to go on thinking about me in the worst way as long as he was safe, safe from his brother, safe from me, and safe from the truth.

The door to a separate interrogation room opened, and two deputies filed out. Marissa walked between them, handcuffed and looking defeated. Jeremy, acting as her defense attorney, trailed them.

I rose to my feet at the sight of my friend and didn't bother to think about the fact that I may never refer to her in that way again.

"Marissa," I called softly.

She turned, halted, and her eyes grew so cold that I shrank back. I was looking at a stranger.

"I guess we both lost our husbands," she said. "Or do you actually think Gray is going to magically forgive you for shooting his brother right in front of him?"

She laughed in my face. "You did, didn't you? How pathetic."

She laughed again and, at the same time, tried to lunge forward, her hands outstretched toward my neck.

"Get her out of here!"

Gray's voice boomed from the doorway of his office, instantly commanding everyone's attention. The deputies, who had been struggling to hold Marissa back, renewed their efforts and forcefully moved her to the door connecting to the jail.

"Wake up, sleeping beauty," Marissa chanted as she was being led away.

When the door closed behind her, I dropped to my seat and let the tears fall. Jeremy came forward and put a comforting hand on my shoulder.

"I'm sorry, Shannon."

I didn't say anything but listened as the soles of his shoes trailed after Marissa and the deputies.

"Are you all right?"

I looked up to see Gray standing over me. "No."

"Do you feel safe going home?"

I nodded. "No one is after me anymore, Gray."

"Then I'll have Deputy Collins take you home. If they need anything more from you, they'll give you a call."

I stood slowly. "I was hoping you and I could talk."

He shook his head. "Not right now."

"Yes, now. I want to explain."

He rubbed his face with his hands. When he brought his hands down, he was staring at me with brown eyes gone hard.

"For four years, I thought my brother was dead, and tonight, I was reunited with him only to watch him die. I also have to face the fact that everything I believed has been a lie. It's all been going through my head over and over, so right now, I just want some fucking peace."

It couldn't have stung worse if he'd slapped me. I shook off the deputy's jacket, folded it, and placed it in the chair I'd just vacated and then stepped around him.

"I'll be outside when Deputy Collins is ready."

"Shannon, wait," he said on a heavy sigh.

I ignored him and headed out of the station, knowing he wouldn't follow after me. The wall that had been constructed between us four years ago was being reinforced with everything that happened tonight.

Marissa was right. Somewhere in the deep recesses of my mind, I had foolishly expected the two of us to skip happily into the future and leave the dark past behind us as though it never existed.

Wake up, sleeping beauty.

CHAPTER FORTY-THREE

One month later...

I put two plates of food in front of a couple I recognized as regulars, and they looked excited to be getting an afternoon out without the kids. I smiled at them, and it gave me pause to see them smiling back. Day by day, I was learning to get used to the idea that I was no longer Gypsy Bay's pariah.

It would also take me some time to get used to the fact that Marissa would no longer be available for me to talk to or laugh and cry with. She had been charged with two counts of conspiracy to commit murder and two counts of attempted murder. I had visited the county jail many times in an attempt to get her to speak to me, but each time, I was refused. I now knew how frustrated and helpless Gray must have felt that first year he tried getting answers from me.

Not seeing Gray was something else I was trying to get used to. That night Deputy Collins took me home had been the last time I spoke to him. Still, I carried on, wanting to give him the space he needed. Now that the threat of Cody was gone, I'd been able to do what I hadn't been able to do since returning to Gypsy Bay, and that was breathe deeply and think about what it was I planned to do now. For four years, Gray and Cody were all that consumed my thoughts, and it felt odd but very nice to think of myself for once.

So I rested, returned to work at Charlie's, renovated my aunt's home into something a family could call home, and pretended as though life was going to continue on—without Gray.

I'd heard through town gossip that he had Cody buried beside their parents in a ceremony that consisted of only himself and the minister. I wanted so much to call him but didn't know how he felt about me at the moment. Did he resent me? Hate me?

The airy, carefree sound of laughter brought my attention back to the entrance of the restaurant. It had become an annoying habit to look up each time someone came through the door, but the man I'd been waiting to see never showed his face.

By the look of Deputy Leah Collins, I immediately knew it was her day off. Instead of the uniform, she wore a pink top and blue jeans that showed off sexy and trim curves. She looked very relaxed, striding hand in hand with a tall, handsome man to her right and a little boy to her left. Her laughter at something the man had said died a little when she noticed me. Still, the sheen of happiness remained on her face.

I couldn't help the jealousy that came over me. It had been a long time since I had something to laugh about, an even longer time since I felt genuinely happy.

Leah politely excused herself and walked over to me. I set the pitcher of iced tea down and faced her with a hesitant smile.

"Your husband?" I asked, nodding my head toward the

man as he and the boy were being led to a window booth by the hostess.

"Yeah," Leah said. "He got in last week, but now it's a little crowded and overwhelming with the three of us living with his mom. I've been on realtor websites every night looking for a place. Speaking of which, I see you're selling your house."

"I just put up the sign last week."

"Why?"

"The money I can get for it will help me finish my degree. I had to drop out years ago when my aunt was diagnosed with stage-four breast cancer."

"I'm happy for you," Leah said. "And I'm sure she would approve."

I smiled indulgently as the two of us fell into a silence filled with all the questions we both wanted to ask but didn't.

"I came over to congratulate you," she said. "I'd heard your record was expunged, and you were issued an apology from the mayor."

I shrugged. "I'm grateful for having a clean record, but the apology wasn't necessary."

"Yes, it was. You may have gone out of your way to get yourself convicted, but if the department had done its job, you never would have been."

"But Gray would have."

"Maybe."

I shook my head. "I couldn't risk that."

Leah's smile turned sympathetic. "It's okay to ask, you know."

I looked over her shoulder to watch her son playing with his father as they read the menu. "How is he?"

"Like you. He's been keeping himself busy, pretending everything is peachy."

"You should get back to your family."

Leah rolled her eyes before turning to walk away. "He's being just as stubborn as you. It's a wonder how the two of you got together in the first place."

The rest of the day was uneventful, giving me time to think about the future I'd planned for myself, so that by the time I walked out of Charlie's that night, I was genuinely hopeful and too distracted to notice Gray leaning against the hood of his truck, waiting for me. When I realized it was him, dressed in jeans and a navy blue T-shirt, I stopped and actually took a step back.

"Where's your uniform?" I asked by way of greeting.

"I'm off duty."

"Oh."

I pulled my fallen purse strap back up to my shoulder and shifted from one foot to the other, not entirely sure why he was here. One month had passed without a single word from him. He seemed to be avoiding Charlie's like the plague, but I still managed to see him around town. However, other than a fleeting glance or subtle nod, I might as well have been a ghost.

"I went by your house and saw a *For Sale* sign in the front yard."

"That's right."

"What's going on?"

"I'm moving. Aunt Christine had a lot of equity in that house, so I decided to sell it and use the proceeds to rent closer to the city and finish my degree."

He crossed his arms and dipped his head. He looked to be composing himself before raising his head to look at me.

"I'm proud of you."

"Thanks. I would have told you sooner, but we haven't—"

"I know," he cut in. "But I'm here now."

I shrugged. "Yes, you're here now, but what do you want me to say?"

"Tell me how you feel."

"I tried to that night." I started to walk past him to get to my car. "You didn't want to hear it, now good night."

Gray moved away from his truck and took hold of my arm. "Then I'll tell you how I feel. Don't leave me now, Shannon. Sell the house if you want, but don't leave. There are plenty of good schools in the area and rent in the city is so expensive…"

He trailed off, looked away, and cursed. When he faced me again, I was met with raw pain.

"I didn't know how to face you," he said. "Ever since that night, finding out the truth, I didn't know what to say to you. So I stayed away."

"I shot your brother," I said.

"To protect me. Just like you took the blame for what I did that night. You were protecting me."

"There was more to it than that."

He gripped my face between his hands. "Then why? Damn you; you let me think you were a cold-blooded murderer when it was really him who was the murderer. You let me serve you divorce papers when, all along, you'd been innocent."

I tried to look away, but he turned me back, keeping my eyes on him. "I came to that place every chance I could get, begging you to tell me what happened. You could've said something then. Don't you know it killed me every night to think of you in that place? I never would've let you stay in there if there had been the slightest chance—"

"I deserved it."

I felt the tears brimming in my eyes but wouldn't let them fall. I didn't want his sympathy. I didn't want him to cave because of some weak gesture.

"You always loved me, Gray," I continued. "You always wanted me. You said so on our wedding night. I knew that, but I still married you for your money, and I planned to trick you out of some of it. Just like you said, I played whore for you."

"Stop, Shannon."

"It's true! If I had just loved you as much as you loved me that night, hell if I had just left you alone, then—"

"Then nothing," he finished. "Cody and I would have still had our issues. The only difference is you and I wouldn't be together."

The thought of that hurt me more than anything.

He let go of me. "Is that all? Is that the only reason you did it, because of some penance you thought you needed to pay?"

I wiped away one tear that had managed to fall. "Do you remember that rainy night I came to the station to ask you for a ride home?"

He didn't say anything, but I knew his mind was already recalling the details of that night.

"You said I could drive your truck, that it would be faster instead of me giving you directions." I paused because the memory was coming back to me in a wave of pictures. "I didn't want to, but you said it was okay. You said if anything happened—"

He framed my face again and kissed me with what felt like all the passion he'd kept bottled up those years without me. I felt the need and ache reverberate throughout his body as I clung to him.

"I remember," he said, in between kisses. "I remember."

"How are we going to do this?" I asked.

"You're coming home with me," he said, holding me close.

"There's so much that's happened between us."

"I don't care. I should have fought for you back then, and I didn't. I won't make that mistake again, and I won't let you make it."

He pulled back to look down at me, his hands firmly cradling my face. "I love you. I never stopped. I don't care why you married me in the first place; I just care about right now. Right now, do you love me?"

The lights from the diner went off as the manager locked up. Soon, we were bathed in nothing but the clouded light of the moon and the fading lights from the street. But I didn't need the light to see him and the adoration in his eyes. I didn't need the light when I walked into his arms to know he was waiting there for me.

"Yes," I whispered to him and the darkness around us. "Yes, I love you."

He kissed me once more, and I clung to him and his warmth. I then rested my head against his chest and turned it to the side. From where we stood, I could see the forest of trees that surrounded Widow Lake. I no longer regarded it as threatening or felt the presence of someone watching me to do harm. I left the past, the betrayal, and the secrets to the darkness. Maybe in the morning, I could convince Gray to walk the trail with me down to the lake, and there we could start again and finally stand in the light together.

*S*ix years ago…

Gray shut his eyes against the glare of the computer screen and rubbed at them. He needed to go home and continue this tomorrow. His shift had ended hours ago, but he was still here, finishing up paperwork and looking into open cases to see if any leads had come up. Earlier, one of his fellow deputies had walked by his desk on his way out and commented on Gray's self-administered overtime.

"Hey, Spencer, the sheriff is gone for the day; you can stop showing off now."

Gray simply shot him the middle finger and continued with his work. It was no secret his goal was to eventually become sheriff of Gypsy Bay, so, yes, he did work hard. But he had to admit he liked the work, and since there was nobody at home waiting for him, he could focus on the career he wanted to build for himself.

He looked out the window at the rain pouring down, drenching the roads. Maybe it would be a good idea if he headed home just to avoid any flooding. He could always finish his paperwork in the comfort of his home office.

He started to shut down his computer when something outside caught his attention. He squinted through the downpour to notice red taillights fading away and took a look around the station. All the deputies on duty were out on calls and patrols. Arlene, the dispatch operator, and he were the only ones in the building, but someone had just driven away.

The sound of the entrance doors opening and shutting put him on alert. He rose from his seat and headed to the outer room where civilians waited.

"Hello," he called and stopped as soon as he saw her.

"I walked from the diner," she said.

Shannon Hollis dropped the hood of her jacket, but her hair was still wet and clinging to her face. Her eyes were wild and bright as if the feel of rain against her skin excited her.

"I saw you through the window, and I thought maybe someone could give me a ride home," she continued. "Normally, I would walk, but it's too far in the rain, and I can't afford to miss work if I get sick."

He could only nod. What the hell was the matter with him? She was fully clothed and drenched from the rain, but the way she had him spellbound, she may as well have been wearing nothing but a towel and wet from coming out of the shower—his shower. But that was how she always affected him, and for as long as he lived, he'd never be able to explain why.

She took a tentative step forward. "Listen, Deputy Spencer, I want to apologize for the other day when I spilled those drinks on you. I hope I didn't ruin your uniform."

He cleared his throat and spoke up before he could embarrass himself any further. "You didn't. It's fine. I was just about to leave. I can give you a lift."

She smiled. "Thanks."

A few minutes later, they were running to his truck. By the time they climbed in and shut the door, both were laughing and wondering what it was about rain that brought out the childish spirit.

"I'm glad I was here when you came by," he said, turning to her in the dark cab. "I'd hate to think of you stranded in this weather."

"I'm glad you were too."

She returned his look, her eyes still gleaming, and he wondered what she would do if he kissed her right now. But he didn't. Instead, he turned and opened the driver's side door again.

"Let's switch. I'll come around, and you can move across to this side."

He didn't give her a chance to argue but got out and ran to the passenger side. She was already in the driver's seat, frowning at him when he climbed back in.

"You want me to drive?"

"You know the way to your aunt's house better than I do. Besides, I trust you to take us where we need to go."

She stared out at some spot beyond the falling rain and swaying trees. "You really shouldn't."

"Shouldn't what?"

"Trust me."

"Why?"

"Because you're such a good person, and I...I might run us into a ditch or something."

He surmised they were talking about more than just driving his pickup, but he'd go along with it.

"Okay, if something happens, I'll just say I was driving."

She turned to him again in surprise. "You'd do that? You'd take the blame for me?"

He shrugged. "Sure."

"You hardly know me, Gray."

"I know you well enough to know you'd do the same for

me." He chuckled. "Besides, it's an old truck anyway. She can take a beating."

She didn't say anything but stared at him for such a long time with those soft brown eyes, he couldn't take it anymore. He wrapped one arm around her waist, pulled her close to him, and kissed her the way he'd fantasized since the day he met her. The sensation of the cold rain against her warm sensuous lips was enough to send him over the edge. But she didn't deserve to be fucked in a pickup truck. He wanted Shannon Hollis completely to himself, and he would have her, just not tonight.

He slowly ended the kiss, pulled his arm from around her waist, and moved away. She kept her eyes closed as though she were trying to keep the memory of him on her lips.

When she opened them, she smiled. "I suppose I would do the same for you."

She then faced forward in her seat, turned the ignition, and steered them toward town.

* * *

Thank you for reading EXILED! If you enjoyed Gray and Shannon's exciting love story, you'll love the next book in the EX FILES series, EXCHANGE.

Sophie's childhood crush is all grown up and irresistible as ever. But is he a murderer?

Here's a sneak peek:

* * *

"You're going to stay with him, aren't you?"

"Ethan."

"Just tell me the truth. Tell me that is exactly what you

plan to do, so that I can walk away from you and quit hoping for something that's never going to happen."

She was looking at him, and he could see in her eyes she was silently pleading for him to stop.

"I told you I don't know what I'm going to do."

"That night he introduced us. How do you think I felt, sitting across from the two of you?"

"I can't talk about this with you."

"I was having dinner with my partner while remembering the days and nights you and I had together."

The air seemed to still around them.

"That was so long ago, Ethan. It was just one summer."

"So that's it? That's all I get is one summer?"

"Yes. It ended there."

"That's not good enough."

He was upon her now, and he knew she saw what was in his eyes. However, she didn't back up. They met in the middle of the kitchen, and as he took hold of her arm, she tried to raise her hand to slap him. He stopped her hand in midair and took hold of her other arm. The mug of tea she was holding crashed to the floor and they began to struggle with each other.

"Stop it, Sophie!"

"I'm so angry with you," she shouted.

"I know."

"I hate him!"

"I know, and it's all right, but I'm not going to fight with you." He was grasping both of her arms and shaking her to get her attention. "I don't want to hurt you."

She stopped trying to hit him and allowed her body to go still. She looked up at him and he saw desperation in her eyes. "Then why did you come here? Why do you keep making me remember?"

They stood there together amid broken shards and spilled

tea, and he knew she was sharing the same memory of the past and remembering how simple it had been. How it had just been the two of them. Before Jason.

He couldn't help it. The look she gave him sent him back to the innocent and vibrant woman she had been when she allowed him to have her. He had to kiss her. He had to keep remembering. He took her in his arms and his lips swept over her full mouth. She tasted so good, so familiar. Every curve and inch of her he'd tried to commit to memory years ago but couldn't hold onto. Now, he was reacquainting himself with her arms, waist, and hips. Sophie returned his kisses and roamed her hands up and down his back as though she were doing the same thing. Ethan moaned, backed her up against the cabinets, and lifted her onto the counter. She immediately spread her legs to allow him to stand between them, and the kiss turned even more intense, passionate—and forbidden.

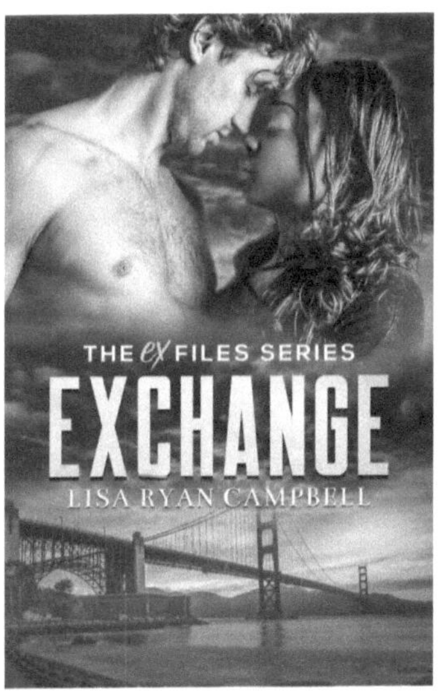

ONE-CLICK EXCHANGE NOW >

"Had me literally sitting on the edge of my seat."

"She has a talent of hooking you from the very beginning."

SIGN UP FOR LISA'S NEWSLETTER:

www.lisaryancampbell.com/newsletter

232

Award-winning Author, Lisa Ryan Campbell began writing as a small child using her mother's pink typewriting paper. Years later, she decided it was important to get a "real job" and attended Arizona State University to major in English with the goal of continuing on for both a Master's and Doctorate degrees in English and teach at the college level.

In 2002, Lisa graduated with a Bachelor's degree in English Literature and an Ancient Egyptian romance novel she wrote in her spare time. She decided then she would not be continuing on to graduate school, but instead joined Romance Writers of America and focused on her true love.

Lisa is an avid traveler and has seen many of the world's treasures in Egypt, Peru, Spain, France, Morocco, England, Mexico and the Caribbean. She spends her time mostly at her home in Colorado writing, reading and watching 1940's noir movies. She also loves to laugh, so you may frequently catch her watching reruns of Archer, Veep and The Office.

Sign up for Lisa's newsletter and find out more about her books at www.Lisaryancampbell.com and connect with her on social media.